The Cat Ate
My Gymsuit

Also by Paula Danziger
in Large Print:

It's An Aardvark-Eat-Turtle World
Divorce Express

The Cat Ate My Gymsuit

Paula Danziger

Thorndike Press • Waterville, Maine

Recommended for Young Adult Readers.

Published in 2005 by arrangement with G. P. Putnam's Sons, a division of Penguin Young Readers Group, a member of Penguin Group (USA) Inc.

The tree indicium is a trademark of Thorndike Press.

The text of this Large Print edition is unabridged. Other aspects of the book may vary from the original edition.

Set in 16 pt. Plantin by Liana M. Walker.

Printed in the United States on permanent paper.

Library of Congress Cataloging-in-Publication Data

Danziger, Paula, 1944–
     The cat ate my gymsuit / by Paula Danziger.
         p. cm.
     Summary: When the unconventional English teacher who helped her conquer many of her feelings of insecurity is fired, thirteen-year-old Marcy Lewis uses her new found courage to campaign for the teacher's reinstatement.
     ISBN 0-7862-7310-0 (lg. print : hc : alk. paper)
     ISBN 0-7862-7267-8 (lg. print : sc : alk. paper)
     1. Large type books. [1. Schools — Fiction.
2. Teachers — Fiction. 3. Large type books.] I. Title.
PZ7.D2394Cat 2005
     [Fic]—dc22   2004027607

To John Ciardi

because he dedicated a book to me,
because he is my good friend
and teacher,
and because he never collects
gin-rummy debts

Chapter 1

I hate my father. I hate school. I hate being fat. I hate the principal because he wanted to fire Ms. Finney, my English teacher.

My name is Marcy Lewis. I'm thirteen years old and in the ninth grade at Dwight D. Eisenhower Junior High.

All my life I've thought that I looked like a baby blimp with wire-frame glasses and mousy brown hair. Everyone always said that I'd grow out of it, but I was convinced that I'd become an adolescent blimp with wire-frame glasses, mousy brown hair, and acne.

My life is not easy. I know I'm not poor. Nobody beats me. I have clothes to wear, my own room, a stereo, a TV, and a push-button phone. Sometimes I feel guilty being so miserable, but middle-class kids have problems too.

Mom always made me go to tap and ballet lessons. She said that they'd make me more graceful. When it came time for the recital, I accidentally sat on the record that I was supposed to dance to, and broke it. I had to hum along with the tap dancing. I sing as badly as I dance. It was a disaster.

Father says that girl children should be born at the age of eighteen and married off immediately.

Stuart, my four-year-old brother, wants to be my best friend so that I can help him put orange pits in a hole in his teddy bear's head.

I'm flat-chested. I used to buy training bras and put tucks in them.

I never had any friends, except Nancy Sheridan. She's very popular, but her mother and mine are PTA officers and old friends, so I always figured that Mrs. Sheridan made her talk to me — Beauty and the Blimp.

School is a bummer. The only creative writing I could do was anonymous letters to the Student Council suggestion box. Lunches are lousy. We never get past the First World War in history class. We never learned anything good, at least not till Ms. Finney came along.

So my life is not easy.

The thing with Ms. Finney is what I want to talk about. She took over for Mr. Edwards, our first English teacher. He left after the first month. One rumor is that he had a nervous breakdown in the faculty lounge while correcting a test on noun clauses. Another is that he had to go to a home for unwed fathers in Secaucus, New Jersey. I personally think that he realized that he was a horrible teacher, so he took a job somewhere as a principal or a guidance counselor.

When Mr. Edwards left, we got a whole bunch of substitutes. None of them lasted more than two days. That'll teach the school to group all the smart kids in one class. We were indestructible.

The entire class dropped books, pencils, and pens at an assigned time. Someone put bubble gum in the pencil sharpener. Nancy pulled her fainting act. We made up names and wrote them on the attendance list. All the desks got turned around. Mr. Stone, the principal, kept coming in and yelling.

And then Ms. Finney came.

Chapter 2

Celeste Sanders was the first to spread the news.

"Hey, we got a new English teacher. A real one, not a sub. First-period class says she looks like a kid."

"A new one. Let's walk in backwards."

"Everyone give a wrong name."

"Let's show her who's boss."

Everybody rushed down the halls and into class. Some of the guys started to make and throw paper airplanes. Alan Smith played "Clementine" on his harmonica. He'd learned it from the instructions on a Good and Plenty box. Jim Heston played the Good and Plenty box, and Ted Martin played a comb. There was applause and cheering after the performance. At 1:15 the coughing started. A few kids didn't do anything, but I did. I really didn't like what was happening, but if you're a blimp with fears of impending acne, you go along with the crowd.

Ms. Finney just sat there. She was young and wore a long denim skirt, a turtleneck jersey and had on weird jewelry — giant earrings that hung down to her shoulders, and a macrame necklace. She didn't smile or yell or cry or read a paper or do any of the things that teachers normally do when a class gets out of hand. She just sat there and looked at everybody.

Finally it got quiet. Everyone started to squirm. It was really creepy after a while.

"O.K. Give her a chance," someone muttered.

We all looked around to see who was talking. It was Joel Anderson, the smartest kid in the class. When almost everybody else would be fooling around, he would sit there reading a book. Some of the kids thought he was a little weird, but everybody usually listened to him.

He put his book down, looked at Ms. Finney, and said, "Are you going to teach us anything?"

Somebody giggled.

The class got very quiet.

I looked at Joel and thought how brave and smart and cute he was. We'd been in the same classes since kindergarten, but I hadn't said more to him than "Hi" and "What's the homework assignment?" I didn't like to embarrass anyone by having them be seen talking to me.

Ms. Finney stood up, looked at the class, smiled, turned to the blackboard, picked up a piece of chalk, and wrote:

"Ms. Barbara Finney."

Turning around again, she smiled and said, "That's my name. I'm your new English teacher, and I hope this year is going to be a good one for all of us."

I thought about that. First of all, she'd written "Ms." Was she just trying to be sharp, or was she really into it? And she'd written her first name. Teachers never do that. They never admit to having first names. They're always Miss or Mr. or Mrs., hardly ever Ms., and never with first names. It's supposed to be a big mystery, like do teachers really have to go to the bathroom or do anything but teach and go to meetings?

She spoke again.

"I decided to be an English teacher because I care about people communicating with people. That's why I'm here. I want to do it and help you all to do it too, as effectively as possible. A poet named Theodore

Roethke once said, 'Those who are willing to be vulnerable move among mysteries.' Please, let's try to move among mysteries together."

The class looked at her and at one another.

Alan Smith laughed and said, "What is this gonna be, a class of detectives?"

Ms. Finney looked at him without smiling. But she didn't yell, either.

"I know that this may all seem a little strange to you now. Maybe it won't work, but let's try. Take out a piece of paper, and for the rest of the period think about communication and write about what it means to you."

We all took out paper. I stared at mine and then snuck looks at Ms. Finney. She was young and pretty and seemed nice. She sounded smart. She was different, but I wasn't sure how, and I didn't know if I could trust her. I mean, she was a teacher, and an adult.

During one of my looks, she stared right at me and smiled. I lowered my head and pretended to be writing. Dumb teacher. Who did she think she was? What does a blimp know about communication? How could she know what it feels like to be so fat and ugly that you're ashamed to get

13

into a gymsuit or talk to skinny people? Who wants to say, "This is my friend, the Blimp"?

Class was almost over, and I still hadn't written anything. I stared at my paper again and began:

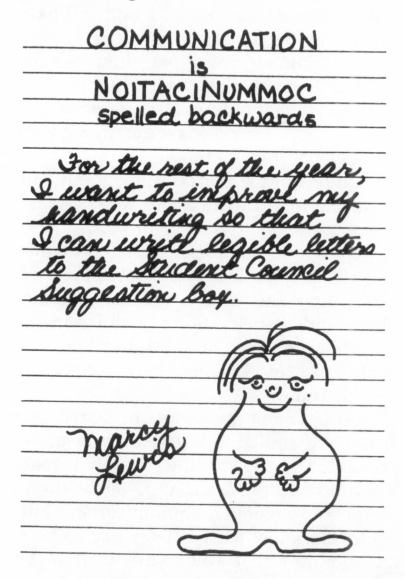

COMMUNICATION
is
NOITACINUMMOC
spelled backwards

For the rest of the year, I want to improve my handwriting so that I can write legible letters to the Student Council Suggestion Box.

The bell rang. Grabbing my books, I rushed up to the front and put my paper face down on the desk. No one else was going to see what I wrote or drew.

Going to gym class, I overheard some of the kids talking about Ms. Finney.

"She seems O.K."

"Weird."

"I like her."

"She's a creep, like the rest of 'em."

In the locker room all the girls rushed to get dressed, except for me. I sat on a bench.

Nancy came over and said, "Marcy, not again! You'll flunk."

I just sat there. Trying to change into a gymsuit while hiding my mini bra and fat body would have been a gymnastic feat in itself.

Once the class started, I walked up to the gym teacher, Schmidt.

"All right, Lewis. What is it this time?"

"The cat ate my gymsuit."

She shook her head, frowned, and wrote another zero in her marking book.

I sat down to watch my eighty-millionth volleyball game.

Chapter 3

Things got better at school after that, at least for me. For a while, some of the kids were mad at Joel for spoiling their fun. But a lot of the kids were glad that everything had settled down. And we started doing some really neat things in class. There was a lot of writing, but I like to do that. Sometimes it is easier to write things down than it is to say them out loud. Ms. Finney said that to communicate is to begin to understand ourselves and others. She wanted us to be honest in our thinking, and to write well. That's really hard, to be honest and remember things like commas and paragraph structure and stuff like that.

The really nice part is that she never asked us to discuss anything that she wouldn't discuss herself. One day we had to write about the things that bothered us.

Ms. Finney stood in front of the class and said, "I remember that when I was a kid, I used to be so embarrassed because I wore braces on my teeth and everyone used to call me 'Tinsel Tooth.' "

That may not sound important, her telling us that, but it made it easier for us to write about and discuss things that bothered us. You know, like mothers who insist on being Girl Scout leaders when you don't even want to be a Girl Scout; falling down steps when you are trying to make an entrance; bad breath; having to take your younger brother to the movies; aunts and uncles who keep asking if many people "shoot up" marijuana; dumb stuff like that. It surprised me how many people had problems. I'm sure that lots of people had more trouble than we talked about, but Ms. Finney was careful not to let it get too personal.

One time, she talked about some guy named Marshall McLuhan, who wrote about people getting turned on by music and films and stuff. Then Ms. Finney turned off all the lights, put on a whole lot of light boxes that blinked on and off, turned on an album real loud, and told us to experience it. She said she wanted us to decide for ourselves whether this type of thing was an escape or a way to really get involved. It was really neat, but then the vice-principal, Mr. Goldman, walked in and called Ms. Finney out of the room. When she came back in, she looked very upset and put the lights back on and stopped the lesson.

We also put on a play. Ms. Finney asked me to be assistant director. That was very hard for me. I had to get up and walk around the room and get stuff ready. I always feel safer sitting behind the desk, where nobody can see my body. But Ms. Finney asked, and it would have been hard for me to explain to her why I didn't want to do it, so I did it. It ended up being O.K.

Don't get me wrong. Ms. Finney wasn't perfect. She never got reports back on time, she gave hard tests, and once in a while she got mad. She also did weird things like holding on to a piece of chalk, forgetting what it was, and trying to smoke it. Sometimes she let kids get away with too much. But she really tried.

And we all really dug her. In the beginning, some of the kids were worried because they were afraid they wouldn't learn what they had to know to pass the college entrance exams. Other kids thought that Ms. Finney was just plain weird. But eventually we all said that we did learn. We wrote more for her than we had ever written before. She never gave true-false or multiple-guess tests. I think most teachers like them because they're easier to correct. Instead, she made us write our own interpretation of what we'd read.

She brought in all kinds of books to read. And a lot of us bought paperbacks from the book club. It was like a celebration the day the books came in the mail and Ms. Finney sorted them out and gave them to us. I spent most of my allowance on books. We shared and swapped them. I feel like I'm addicted to the printed word. Like I need a book fix when I get upset.

We talked about poetry and current events and plays and movies. Ms. Finney knew an awful lot, and she made us feel that we knew a lot too and were important. She really listened. It was amazing.

And she didn't talk to us just in English class. During her free periods she'd walk around the school and drop in on some classes, like home ec. and shop and art, classes where there were times that she wouldn't be interrupting other teachers. She'd taste the food that the kids made, admire the sewing, and look at all the projects in shop. It made everybody feel good, like she knew that there was more to us than just the time we spent in her class.

One day she came into my gym class. I had just told Schmidt that my little brother had misplaced his security blanket and was now using my gymsuit instead. Ms. Finney looked at everybody playing volleyball and then came over and sat down next to me.

"Hi, Marcy."

"Hi, Ms. Finney."

"Who's winning?"

"The blue team."

"Don't you feel well?"

"I'm O.K. Why?"

"Just wondered."

We sat and watched the game for a few minutes. I didn't know what else to say.

She turned and said, "I'm going to ask Ms. Schmidt if I can play. I'm a real clod at volleyball, but it's fun. Do you want to play too?"

I shook my head. Looking at me as if she wanted to say something else, she just smiled and walked over to the game. Schmidt obviously said that she could play, because she took off her shoes and joined the red team.

She really was bad. When someone hit the ball to her, she ducked. When she served, she didn't always get it over the net. But she looked as if she were having fun, making up her own rules as she went along.

"It's a do-over. I forgot to call out the score."

"English teachers get an extra serve."

"People named Barbara get two extra serves."

Someone yelled across the net, "Hey, Ms. Finney. Just pretend that the ball is a direct object and our team is the indirect object."

Ms. Finney smiled and volleyed. The ball just missed hitting Nancy on the head. Nancy turned around, laughed, and yelled, "She said a direct object, not a dangling participle."

Schmidt blew her whistle and said, "Everyone hurry up. Into the showers and then get dressed."

Ms. Finney yelled, "Thanks, everyone, for letting me play." Then she came over and said, "That was fun."

I just smiled at her and followed the rest of the kids into the locker room.

One day in class, Nancy raised her hand and asked Ms. Finney if we could do more about how we felt inside. Ms. Finney thought about it and said that we had to use the class time to do what was in the syllabus, the guide that schools give teachers. She said that she felt a responsibility to go over the assigned material. After thinking awhile, she smiled and said, "Why don't we start a club after school? That'll work. I'll tell my other classes and you all tell other friends. We'll start Monday after school."

That's how Smedley got started.

Chapter 4

Smedley wasn't a person. It was the club. What happened was that twenty-five kids came, which was really good because a lot of the kids had to take buses to school and staying after meant a long walk or having someone pick you up. We figured that the club should have a name. Nancy suggested "The Self Club." Joel wanted it to be called "Interpersonal Persons." Alan Smith said that we should be named "The Sherlock Holmes Crew," because we all would be searching to find ourselves. That kid is probably going to be a detective some day, or a peeping tom. A kid from another class said, "Why don't we just call ourselves Smedley, after that dopey guy in our grammar book who is always looking for the right way to say things?" Everyone liked that.

Ms. Finney said that we should begin by

examining what had just happened, that each of us should look at how we acted in the group and how we all finally agreed. This, she said, was group dynamics in action. She said that she had taken college courses involving that sort of thing, and that she had had a minor in something called Human Organizational something or other. I don't remember exactly, but it sounded good.

So we talked about it and saw that some people have different roles in a group. Some are leaders. Some are reactors. (Alan thought that meant that he was like an atomic reactor.) Joel said that Alan and Robert Alexander always acted like clowns when they wanted attention or were afraid of something. They both got mad at him and called him a brainy creep. He called them cretins, and finally Ms. Finney had to tell them to stop.

"O.K. That's enough. If you want me to be advisor to this club, you all have to try to work things out. Let's begin with an exercise to get acquainted."

Nancy raised her hand and said, "Ms. Finney. That's silly. We've known each other since kindergarten."

Ms. Finney looked around the room. "You may have known each other since kindergarten, but do you really know each other? I bet you don't. I've noticed that some of you don't even talk to people who aren't in your classes."

She split us up into pairs and told us to spend fifteen minutes getting to know the other person. I thought I was going to die. She had put Joel and me together.

Joel pulled his desk near mine and said, "Hi. I'm Joel Anderson."

I just nodded my head.

"You should tell me your name now."

How could I tell him? I was so nervous, I couldn't remember anything. Finally, it came to me.

"Hi. I'm Marcy Lewis."

Joel asked, "Have you always lived here?"

Again I nodded my head. I couldn't stand it. I felt like such a blob, a real idiot.

Joel tried again. "What would you like to tell me about yourself?"

I didn't know. Was I supposed to tell him I was a blimp trying to disguise myself as a real person; or that I probably had a horrible case of contagious impending pimples; or that I had this weird brother with a teddy bear filled with orange pits; or that I thought that he was cute and brave and probably thinking about how suicide would be better than talking to me?

I finally looked down at my desk and said, "I'm Marcy Lewis . . . thirteen . . . I hate dancing lessons . . . grammar tests . . . and questions."

He said, "Don't you like anything?"

I thought for a while and said, "Yeah. I like Ms. Finney, reading books . . . and felt-tip markers."

Then I sat there, trying to think of something, anything, to ask him.

"Joel, do you like Ms. Finney?"

"Yes. I do."

"Were you scared when you got mad at the class and told them to give her a chance?"

"Why should I be scared saying what I believe?"

"Aren't you afraid that people won't like you?"

Joel just looked at me. I decided that I'd better change the subject.

"Do you have any brothers or sisters?" I asked.

"No."

"What do you want to be when you grow up?"

"Joel Anderson."

Ms. Finney told the class to pull the desks into a circle, and that each of us had to introduce our partner to the group. Everybody seemed to know new things about the others. When my turn came, I said, "This is Joel Anderson. He doesn't have any brothers, sisters, or pets, and I think he's smart." Then I sat back and waited for Joel to introduce me.

"This is Marcy Lewis. She says that she doesn't like lots of things, but I bet she really does . . . and she has a nice smile."

I couldn't believe it. I'd been sure he was going to say something like "This is Marcy Lewis. She's a real creep and doesn't know how to talk." Or "This is Marcy. She might even look human if she didn't look like a Mack truck." I wasn't used to anyone saying anything nice, except Nancy and my mother, because they had to.

Once we had finished with all the introductions, Ms. Finney told us all to reach out to the people at the desks on either side of us, hold hands, close our eyes, and think about the group. Joel was on one side of me, Ms. Finney on the other. All I could think about was how scared I was that my hands were sweaty. I was also afraid that they would notice that my fingernails were all bitten down.

The group sat like that for a long time. Then everybody sort of let go, and Ms.

Finney said that we should all go home and write a self-description to bring in for the next week, one that only she would read.

I was afraid to look at Joel. All of a sudden, I heard him say, " 'Bye, Marcy. See you in class tomorrow." He had talked to me in front of all those people! I was so excited, but I just smiled and said, "Yeah. See ya, Joel."

Nancy and I walked home, Beauty and the Blimp, Wonderwoman and the Blob Who Ate Brooklyn. Nancy was really excited about Smedley. She kept saying how much fun it would be, how she liked to get to know people, and how she thought it would be good for me. I asked her why.

"Oh, Marcy. You know. You're so hung up about your weight . . . you and your family don't talk to each other . . . and you're so afraid of things . . . and you shouldn't be."

I just clumped along, biting my nails and thinking about what she had said.

Chapter 5

School went on as usual. I kept getting good grades in everything but gym. My anonymous letters to the Student Council suggestion box were ignored. Lunches continued to be lousy. We were only up to the Civil War in history class.

It was different in some ways, though. I didn't sit alone at lunch anymore. I sat with some of the kids from Smedley. Ms. Finney's classes were still great, but the rest of the classes seemed even more boring than they were before she came. We kept asking the teachers to be more like her, but they made faces and told us to keep quiet. We talked out in classes more and asked more questions, but they didn't like that. We even asked some of them to join Smedley, but they said things like "What are you doing? Getting your heads shrunk?" and "My contract doesn't say I have to stay after school past last period."

What changed a lot was my home. It got even worse. My father has a horrible temper. He doesn't hit, but he yells. Even worse, he says awful things to me, like "I don't care if you get good grades. You do stupid things. Why do I have to have a daughter who is stupid and so fat? I'll never get you married off."

My mother would try to tell him to stop, but he wouldn't listen. They'd get into a fight and she'd start to cry and then go get a tranquilizer.

Then my little brother, Stuart, would cry and run for his teddy bear. While all this was happening, my father would scream at me. "Look at what you've done. We'd never fight if it weren't for you. Apologize." By that time, I'm crying. It usually ended with me running upstairs, slamming my door, throwing myself on my bed, and rocking back and forth. My mother would come in and hug me and tell me everything would be O.K., but that I really should lose some weight and look like everyone else.

I hated it. That's what usually went on in my house but, as I said, things got much worse.

In a way, it was because of Smedley. We did lots of neat stuff in there, and I wanted to try some of it at home.

One day in Smedley we broke up into small groups and told each other how we saw each other and felt about each other. I was really excited. Nobody said that they hated me. They said I was smart and nice, but too quiet and shy. No one made fun of me. They didn't say I was skinny and beautiful, but they didn't tell me I was ugly and fat either. So I thought that maybe it would be good to try it at home.

My mother was all for it. I had told her about what we were doing in Smedley, and she really dug it, because she said it was making me different. I didn't tell her how scared I still was, though. I wanted her to be proud of me.

So one night at dinner, she explained that she wanted us all to sit around and talk like a family.

My father said, "I've worked hard all day for this family, Lily. Isn't that enough? I don't have to talk to all of you too, do I?"

Mom very quietly said, "Martin, I think it's important. Please."

So he said, "O.K. . . . for a little while."

Mom and I cleared off the dishes, and then we went into the living room, where my father was watching television. Stuart was sitting on the floor, stuffing pits into the hole in Wolf, his teddy bear. Stuart watches a lot of commercials, and he once saw that oranges are supposed to keep you healthy. He used to try to put whole oranges in Wolf, but things got pretty sticky, so we convinced him that pits are best for bears.

My father frowned and said, "No, let the kid stay here. He's part of the family too. And anyway, I want to talk to him about his stupid thumbsucking and that idiot teddy bear."

Stuart held Wolf in his arms and started to suck his thumb. "I love Wolf. He's my friend. He never yells at me."

"Look, kid. You're four years old . . . What are you going to be? Forty, hugging that bear and sucking your thumb? You'll never get a job that way."

Stuart started to cry.

I was scared, but I said, "Daddy. Please don't yell at him. He's just a little kid."

He started to yell. "Don't you start. First I have problems at work. And then I have to come home to all this. All I want is a little peace and quiet. I was an only child. I'm not used to all the noise in the house. Your mother is always busy with you two.

She never has enough time for me."

My mother said, "Martin. Please calm down." He kept it up. Stuart started to cough really hard. I started to shake. I didn't want to show him that I was upset, but then I yelled, "You don't want to talk because you think I'll say that I hate you."

"I don't care if you hate me. Don't you ever talk to me that way, young lady. Go up to your room."

"Martin. Give her a chance to talk. You don't give anyone a chance to say anything."

"You just keep quiet. What do you mean, I don't give anyone a chance to talk?"

"That's exactly what I mean."

My father stood up and yelled, "Marcy! This is all your fault. You and that stupid group-dynamics crap. Why can't you leave well enough alone."

I screamed, "I hate you! Just leave me alone," and ran up to my room. I could still hear them fighting. Crying, I heard the door open. It was Stuart, with Wolf.

"Can I come in?"

"O.K." I tried to stop crying.

He sat on the bed. "Marcy. I love you. Wolf loves you. Don't cry. Please."

"Stuart. I love you too."

"Why is everybody always yelling? Why

can't we be happy?"

"Don't worry. It'll be all right."

"I don't like yelling."

We just held on to each other. My mother came in and said, "Daddy doesn't mean anything when he yells. That's just his way. Don't be frightened. He loves you very much. He just doesn't know how to show it."

I could see that she had been crying. I felt so bad. Nothing that I ever did turned out right.

"Your father says that he's sorry and that we should go shopping Saturday and buy you some new clothes. He thought you'd like that."

"I don't want his dumb money for clothes."

"Please, Marcy. Be reasonable. He's sorry."

"I hate him."

"Please don't say that. You're upsetting me."

So we stopped talking about it. Stuart and I went downstairs, and Mom gave us large bowls of ice cream. My father walked into the kitchen. Stuart started sucking his thumb. I finished up my ice cream and asked for more.

"Marcy. Did your mother tell you that

you are both going shopping?"

"Yes."

"Buy anything you want." Then he walked out of the room.

When I went to bed that night, I thought about how bad it was in my house, how much I loved Stuart, and how glad I was that Smedley and Ms. Finney were at school.

Chapter 6

English class was really good. We worked hard, but it was fun.

Certain things were always the same. Every Monday we had to hand in compositions. Wednesday we took our spelling tests, and then there were "The Finney Friday Flicks." We could bring in popcorn while we watched the movies. After seeing the films, we discussed them.

Book-report times were great. Once we had to come to school as a character in the book that we'd read. It was like the thing in Smedley, only we were the characters, not ourselves. Getting into small groups, we talked about who we were and what happened in our lives. Then we joined with the other groups and introduced one another. It seemed as if the characters from the books were real people.

Another time, after studying what propaganda is all about, we made up one-minute television commercials to "sell" our book. We videotaped each one with the school's equipment, and after watching all of them we talked about how they worked or didn't work.

Writing a children's book was another assignment. First we talked about what kinds of things were important, like plot, theme, time, place, and stuff like that. Then we each wrote a story and gave it to Ms. Finney to be typed up. After that we illustrated them. She taught us how to bind them into books. When we finished, she tried to get school time off to use our books in a special project. But Stone wouldn't give it to us, so we met on a Saturday at our town hospital. We visited little kids who were sick, read our stories to them, and then left the books there so that the hospital would always have books for the kids to read. Some of the class even asked for and got permission to visit every Saturday.

Another time, we talked about humor, satire, and parody. We decided to write our own television show, and called it *Dr. Sickbee at Your Service*. It was the story of an orthodontist who moonlights in a rock band, lives next door to a weird family, has a younger sister who ran away to join the roller derby, and solves mysteries in his spare time. We put it on videotape and picked out the best of the book commercials to use with it, and some of the other English teachers let their classes see it.

Once we had to learn a list of literary terms, vocabulary and spelling words, and parts of speech. I spent a whole weekend studying because I figured that the test was going to be a killer. Getting to class, we saw that Ms. Finney had made up a large game board that read "This Way to Tenth Grade." Each row was a team. We rolled a die and landed on one of the categories. If we answered correctly, we got to stay there. If not, we had to go back. There were all sorts of penalty cards, like "Missed the bus," "Wait one turn," "Your locker is messy. Lose two turns cleaning it," "Talking during assembly. Go back three steps." The first team to make it to the end graduated to tenth grade.

Another time, we walked in and there was a weird-looking guy standing with Ms. Finney. He wore a trenchcoat and a cap, and had a pipe.

"Class. I'd like to introduce you to my

friend, Sherlock Houses, the defective detective."

"Hi, kids. I have a problem, and Ms. Finney says that you're pretty smart and can help me. You see, I'm working on The Case of the Missing Drummer."

"I'd rather work on The Case of the Missing Beer."

"Cool it, Robert," said Ms. Finney with a smile.

Sherlock continued. "The kidnappers left a ransom note. But I accidentally spilled coffee on it, and some of the words are blurred. Could you help me figure it out?"

We groaned but agreed to play their game, and Sherlock and Ms. Finney handed out copies of the note with certain words messed up. We spent the rest of the period trying to figure out the missing words.

At the end of the period, Ms. Finney told us that Sherlock was really a friend of hers from graduate school and that what we had done was an exercise in understanding words in context.

It was fun.

Chapter 7

We should have guessed that Smedley and Ms. Finney were too good to last. There were all sorts of clues. We noticed that the principal came in to observe quite often. But they sometimes do that with new teachers. We were extra good when he was there. After all, it was Ms. Finney's first year as a teacher, and we saw that she got kind of nervous when someone came in to check her out. So we tried to remember to raise our hands and wait to be called on. Ms. Finney always said hand raising wasn't necessary if we all respected one another.

One day Mr. Stone walked in, sat down in the back, and put his clipboard down on the desk.

We had been working when he came in, but everyone stopped.

Ms. Finney said, "Let's continue. Who

knows what images are used in this story?"

Seven hands were raised. Robert Alexander waved his.

"All right. Give one example, Robert."

"He's stubborn as a mule. That's a metaphor."

Thomas Shaw yelled, "No, that's a simile."

Ms. Finney said, "Who's right? Joel, do you know?"

"It's a simile," Joel answered. "A comparison of two dissimilar things using *like* or *as*."

"Very good. Now, Robert. Try to find a metaphor."

"O.K. . . . How about 'The room is a pigsty'?"

"Very good," said Ms. Finney.

We were real careful to do our best. We didn't answer more questions than we would have, but we didn't laugh as much, and it just wasn't as much fun. But we all knew that things like that are important to principals. I think that at Principals' School they are taught to look for things like raising hands, checking hall passes, making sure that the window shades are at a certain level, and making announcements over the loudspeaker that begin "This is your principal speaking. I must have your attention please." Anyway, Mr.

Stone must have gotten A's in all these areas.

So we tried hard that day. When Ms. Finney asked Robert Alexander to use "philosophy" in a sentence, he said, "The derivation of that philosophy obviously was influenced by a group of loquacious siblings." It made no sense, but it sounded erudite (another word that Ms. Finney had us look up).

When Mr. Stone left, Ms. Finney laughed and said, "Look, don't try so hard. Just be yourself."

Robert said, "I thought Mr. Stone would be impressed. That's how he sounds at school assemblies."

"But your sentence didn't make much sense."

"That's why he'd like it."

Then Ms. Finney picked up a piece of chalk and wrote a quote from Shakespeare, something about sound and fury signifying nothing. Sometimes she got into stuff that's hard to understand, but maybe someday I'll put it all together.

Two weeks later, we came into class and found a substitute.

Chapter 8

We figured that Ms. Finney must be sick or taking a mental-health day to recuperate from teaching us.

The substitute made us diagram sentences on the blackboard. Halfway through the period, Mr. Stone walked into the class, stood in front of us, cleared his throat, and said, "Miss Finney will probably not be returning to this school. Mrs. Richards will be here until we find a new full-time English teacher. Now get back to work."

Get back to work, he said. How could we do that?

Alice Carson raised her hand and asked, "Mr. Stone. Is Ms. Finney all right? Is she sick . . . or in an accident . . . What happened?"

Mr. Stone looked at us. "Miss Finney

will no longer be a teacher in my school. I want all of you to forget everything she taught you."

The room was very still for a minute. Then Joel stood up and said, "Ms. Finney taught me the proper methods of punctuation. Should I forget that?"

Mr. Stone got even madder. Turning to Joel and glaring, he said, "Joel Anderson, you're a troublemaker. Detention for the rest of the month."

Before I even realized what I was doing, I stood up and said, "Ms. Finney is the best teacher in the whole dumb school, and I want her back again."

Mr. Stone looked shocked. "Marcy Lewis! This isn't at all like you. Now sit down and keep quiet."

I was sick of hearing that. First my father and now Mr. Stone. So I kept standing there, and said, "You have not converted a man because you have silenced him." That was a quotation that Ms. Finney had had us write about.

The whole class applauded.

Mr. Stone said, "You all have detention, and Marcy, this is not like you. Your mother is president of the PTA. She will be very upset when she hears about this."

The bell rang. He told us to go to our

next class. We didn't move.

"I said, go to your next class. You will be very sorry. I will put this on your school records."

He stormed out of the room, and we heard him screaming at some kid who was at his locker at an unassigned time.

We still hadn't moved. Some of the kids started to cry. I did. My whole world seemed upside down.

Joel finally spoke. "Come on. Let's go. We're not helping ourselves or Ms. Finney. Let's find out what's happening."

Everyone got up to leave. Joel came over to me and said, "Marcy. You were great. You really told that fool off. I'll see you in detention, and we'll figure out what we're going to do." Then he left.

I didn't believe it. Joel spoke to me and said that he liked what I did!

Nancy stood there and said, "You really did it. I'm glad."

We had to run to the gym. Nancy didn't want to be late. I didn't care. When we got to gym, I went up to the gym teacher and told her that I had been mugged on the way to school by a syndicate specializing in stolen gymsuits. Then I sat down and watched another thrilling volleyball game.

The day went quickly. I called up my

mother and told her that I was staying after to do something extra with my English class. I didn't mention that the something extra was detention. That would have been tranquilizer territory. She was pleased, and said, "Marcy, I'm so glad that you are getting involved in school activities."

After the last class, Nancy and I rushed to the bathroom. She combed her hair and I checked for pimples. Then we headed for detention.

Joel was standing by the door. He smiled when he saw us, and said, "We'd better hurry up. They give added time if we're late."

So the three of us sat down in the back.

Nancy whispered, "What do you think is happening?"

Joel said, "I don't know, but my Dad is on the Board of Education. I'll try to find out."

I whispered, "It must be something awful. They usually let teachers at least finish out the year."

"Maybe she starred in an X-rated film and Mr. Stone saw it." That was Nancy's idea.

The detention teacher kept looking at us. Joel told us that we had to quiet down or else we would have to stay later. He and

Nancy had had detention before, but this was all new to me.

I sat there and pretended to read. Usually it's easy for me to read, but this time I was so upset that I couldn't do anything.

The teacher finally told us that time was up and we could go. Everyone rushed out of the room.

"Marcy, I'm going to ask my father what's happening. I'll let you know as soon as I find out. Then you can call Nancy and she can let some other kids know."

"O.K. Please find out. Joel, do you think it's really bad? I'm scared."

Joel shrugged and shook his head. "I don't know," and then he walked away.

Nancy and I headed home.

"Hey, Marcy, what are we going to do if she can't come back? What happens to English class and to Smedley? They won't let us have Smedley without a teacher."

I could feel the tears coming down my face. I couldn't say anything.

Nancy stopped and grabbed my hand. "Don't cry. It'll be all right." She thought for a minute. "I take that back. Ms. Finney says it's good to show emotions. Marcy, go ahead. Cry if it makes you feel better."

That's why it was all so important to me.

The kids from Smedley and Ms. Finney still cared about me even if I showed my feelings. I felt as if someone had taken a vacuum cleaner and cleaned all my insides out and left me with only my blimp outside.

"Marcy, I think Joel likes you. He said he was going to call you tonight, not me, and he's been talking to you a lot lately."

I guess Nancy told me that because she thought it would make me feel better. But it didn't.

Chapter 9

When I got home, my mother was waiting for me at the door.

"Honey, what happened at school today? Mr. Stone called and was very upset."

"Did you have to take a tranquilizer?"

"Oh, Marcy, don't be mean. I can't help it. You know things aren't easy for me."

I knew that. I mean, her husband is related to me too. And she also worried about me and Stuart.

"Mom, I get scared that you use them too much. In school they say that prescriptions shouldn't be abused."

"I'm careful. Look, Marcy, what happened?"

So I told her about what had happened. I started to cry when I got to the part about Ms. Finney and Smedley. She held me.

"Honey, do you love Miss Finney more than me?"

"No . . . It's different. She's not afraid, and she's helping me not to be afraid. And she teaches good stuff in class. It's not fair. Mr. Stone is an idiot."

"Oh, honey, don't talk like that."

"It's true. He's an idiot, a dope. He's just rotten."

"Marcy, he's a human being. Remember that."

"Nothing you say can make me believe that. Stone's not human. There's not one nice thing about him."

"You know, Marcy, life's not like that. No one is all bad or all good — not Mr. Stone, not your father, not me, no one. You've got to learn that."

I just shook my head. "Stone's a fool."

Just then, Stuart came running into the house. He'd been riding his bike, and had fallen. We ran over to him.

"Stuart, where does it hurt?"

He just kept crying.

My mother looked for broken bones and blood. Finding none, she said, "I think you'll live. Did you break the sidewalk?"

Stuart shook his head.

"Would you two like some ice cream?"

We said yes and headed for the kitchen.

"Wolf wants some orange pits."

"We're out of oranges. We'll get some later."

I decided to say something. "Stuart, I love you."

He smiled, and I smiled back. It's so easy to love him sometimes. He's a little weird, but he's a good person, for a four-year-old. Ms. Finney says that age doesn't matter, but sometimes it's hard to talk to a little kid. But the thing with Stuart is that we say a lot without talking.

We heard a car door slam, a scary sound when you know that it means your father is home. My mother went to the front door to meet him.

"What a rotten day," he said. That's what he always says. It's always the same. My mother then kisses him and hands him a Scotch and soda. It's one of our few family traditions.

"Martin, I want to talk to you about something. Please, stay calm."

My mother has a fantastic sense of timing. It got quieter, and then I heard my father scream, "Marcy Lewis, get in here!"

I ran into the living room and tripped on

the rug, but didn't fall.

"You're such a klutz. I thought sending you to dancing school was supposed to make you more graceful."

"I wanted drum lessons, not dancing."

"You'd probably give yourself a concussion with the drumsticks," my father said. "What's this I hear about school?"

"Mr. Stone's wrong. Ms. Finney's a good teacher."

"How many times must I tell you to respect your elders?"

"But he's wrong."

"I doubt that, but even if he were, you must learn to respect those in authority. How do you expect to get ahead?"

"I don't care about that. All I care about is Ms. Finney."

"I never did like her, young lady. She's been feeding you a lot of garbage, with that sensitivity-training crap and calling herself Ms. What's wrong with Miss? Just be good and play by the rules and you'll be a much happier person. Your mother and I know that."

"Martin, I think Miss Finney has helped Marcy."

"Don't you start. Look. I know what's best for this family. Don't I support you and take care of you?"

Stuart came over, hugged me, and smiled.

"Why is the kid so dirty?" my father asked.

"I fell off my bike," Stuart remembered.

"Just what we need. Another clumsy kid in this family."

My mother said, "Let's all wash up for dinner. Marcy and Stuart, let's go set the table."

We went into the kitchen while my father sat down to read the paper in the living room.

Once the table was set and dinner ready, we all sat down. My father talked about how hard his job was. Stuart kept sucking his thumb. I stared at my plate, and my mother suggested how nice it would be for all of us to go on a weekend trip.

"I work hard all week," my father said. "I want to relax on the weekends."

Everything got so quiet, you could hear the milk going down Stuart's throat. The phone rang. My mother got up to answer it. I figured it was Mr. Stone again. I got really scared.

"Marcy, it's for you. A young gentleman."

I had forgotten. Joel had said he'd call me if he found out any new developments.

I got up from the table and went to the phone as if I were used to getting calls every day from boys.

"Hi, Marcy. I just found out. It's serious."

"What happened? Did she lose her marking book?"

"Very funny. She's been suspended because she won't say the Pledge of Allegiance in homeroom."

I thought about that for a while.

"But lots of kids don't say it."

"She's not a kid, she's a teacher. And anyway, my father thinks it's more than that. He says a lot of people don't like her — Mr. Stone, some of the teachers, Mr. Goldman, and some of the parents."

"How can't they like her?"

"Look, Marcy, she's different. Not everybody likes you when you act and dress differently."

"Joel, I really care about her. What can we do?"

"I'm not sure. Listen, meet you in front of school tomorrow half an hour before classes start, O.K.?"

"Yeah. Well, I'll see you."

I called Nancy right away, told her what was happening, and had her spread the word. My father was yelling that I'd better get back to the table, so I hung up and went back to the dinner table. As I sat down, my mother started gushing. "Our daughter is growing up . . . her first call from a boy."

My father grumbled, "Can't you tell your little friends not to call during dinnertime?"

"Oh, Martin. It's her first call from a boy. Did he ask you out?"

I couldn't stand it anymore. "Look. I'm sorry he called during dinner. He wanted to know if he can borrow Wolf to cut it up in science class."

Stuart started to cry. Sometimes I feel really sorry for the kid, but it was the only way that I could get my parents to stop bothering me about the call.

"That's it, young lady. Go to your room!" my father screamed.

"Martin. She hasn't finished eating," my mother said softly.

"That's all right. That girl won't waste away to nothing."

I ran upstairs to my room and cried.

A while later, my mother knocked at the door and immediately came in. She didn't even give me time to say whether I wanted company.

"Honey, I'm sorry it's like this. You've got to learn to live with it. I'm sorry. I love you very much."

We hugged each other, and then she left and I cried myself to sleep.

Chapter 10

My alarm went off in the morning. I got up, dressed, and went downstairs. Both my parents were eating breakfast. The morning paper was lying on the table. Ms. Finney's picture was on the front page. The headline read "Junior High Teacher Dismissed; Refuses to Pledge Allegiance."

Miss Barbara Finney, teacher of English at Dwight David Eisenhower Junior High School, has been suspended from her duties until further notice for her refusal to say the Pledge of Allegiance.

Mr. Frank Stone, Principal, stated, "As a good American, I am chagrined to think that this type of individual is allowed to influence impressionable young people."

Miss Finney was not available for comment at publication time.

A hearing will be held on Tuesday, October 15, at 8:00 p.m. in the auditorium of J. Edgar Hoover High School. The public is invited to attend.

Finishing the article, I put the paper back down on the table.

My father started. "I suppose you are impressed by this woman's actions."

"I've learned a lot in her class."

He slammed down his coffee cup. "I want you to stay out of this, Marcy. You are not going to turn into a revolutionary. Learn to play by the rules."

I concentrated on pouring the milk on my cornflakes.

My mother put her hand on mine. "I'm sorry. I was very impressed by her when I met her at the PTA meeting."

I asked, "Can I go to the hearing?"

"Martin. Why don't we go together — you and me and Marcy. I know it's important to her."

"All right. I suppose so. It'll be interesting to see Miss Know-It-All's teacher get fired. But I'm warning you, young lady. I want you to stay out of trouble."

"Can I be excused? I have to meet

someone at school to go over homework."

"All right, but remember what I said."

I ran up to my room, grabbed my books and jacket, and ran out the door before anyone else had a chance to say anything to me.

When I got there, Joel was waiting. A bunch of other kids were also standing around. They were from the different classes that Ms. Finney taught. Also from Smedley. All of them were pretty upset.

Joel said, "What we have to do is get all of the kids together and make plans. Each of you go around now and get lists of kids who are willing to help support her."

The group broke up, and Joel turned to me.

"Marcy, we have only four school days and a weekend before the hearing. We've got to organize fast. And listen, Nancy's decided to have a party Saturday night. Would you go with me?"

Just like that, I got asked out for my very first time.

"Yeah, if you want to take me, I guess I can go. But I have to ask my parents first."

The bell rang for homeroom, and we got up and went into the school. I was in a daze. Joel and I went to our separate lockers. I ran into Nancy.

"Hey, Marcy, you had to hang up last night before I had a chance to tell you. I'm having a party Saturday. Can you come?"

"Yeah. Joel just invited me . . . I think."

"What do you mean, 'I think'?"

"Yeah. He asked me."

"Don't be so surprised. I said he liked you. See?"

Mr. Stone walked up to us. "Good morning, girls. Marcy, I want to see you in my office after homeroom. Be there promptly." Then he walked on.

"Marcy. Are you going to get it because of what happened in class yesterday?"

"Probably. What's it like to go to the principal's office?"

"I don't know. I only get detention a lot."

Just what I needed to think about. Maybe we'd have an earthquake during homeroom and I wouldn't have to go. Or maybe I'd be lucky enough to trip and break my leg so that the ambulance would carry me away before I got to the office. Probably if that happened Mr. Stone would yell and tell me to go to the nurse, who would tell me to take a nap and then go back to class.

Going into homeroom, I tripped over someone's feet, but I didn't break anything.

When it came time to say the Pledge, I looked around to see what everyone was doing. Some kids said it. Others passed chewing-gum sticks and notes. A couple of kids talked. Not too many seemed aware of the words. What did it all mean? It seemed to say everything that Ms. Finney believed in, liberty and justice for all, one nation. Maybe it was the under-God part. She never talked about religion, but maybe that was it. I didn't know.

The bell rang, and I headed for the office. Lots of kids were there. Some had come to school late, and now they were waiting around until the secretary had time to make out late passes. A couple of kids were there because they had been caught sneaking cigarettes in the bathroom. They should have gone to the faculty room. The smoke there is so thick, no one would have seen them. I sat down, chewed on my nails, and waited to see Mr. Stone.

About forty-five minutes later I was called into his office. He had a picture of his family on his desk. It was the kind that you get on a Christmas card with a dittoed letter about how the family was doing and how they had grown. Mr. Stone frowned at me.

"Marcy, you were very rude to me yesterday. I don't understand it. You've always been such a good student. I don't want you or any other student to get involved in this situation. It's a matter for grown-ups to handle."

I was scared, like when you go to the doctor to get a flu shot. But I couldn't let him bully me.

"Mr. Stone, it involves us. Ms. Finney was our teacher, and she's a good teacher."

He kept frowning. "Don't you understand? I'm very concerned. Miss Finney has a great many philosophies and teaching techniques that are not good."

"No, I don't understand."

"Marcy, the younger generation just doesn't understand they've got to play by the rules. Let me tell you about my oldest daughter. She was a good student, just like you, and she was accepted to a fine college. When she got there, she met some people with very radical ideas. Now she's dropped out of school and is living in a commune and spending all her time making quilts and gardening. Can't you see now why I am so concerned about Miss Finney and her strange ways?"

"But, Mr. Stone, she's not strange. She does teach us regular English. And I don't think your daughter is doing anything wrong."

Mr. Stone exploded. "That's it! I've had it! Now you listen, young lady. You'll be very sorry some day. I've spent my whole life trying to keep America's ideals in mind, and this school a good place to educate young people. And then along comes a teacher who talks about feelings and being in touch with yourself and she doesn't believe in grades and argues at teachers' meetings and doesn't dress like a teacher and won't salute the flag. And I also have to deal with community pressure. Well, I just won't have it."

I got really scared. It's horrible to be yelled at. Then his phone rang. He picked it up, listened for a minute, and looked up and said, "Marcy, I hope that you understand that I only want the best for all of you. You may now return to class."

I left the office. I was very confused. I had gotten a late pass to go to gym. As long as Mr. Stone kept me out of class, he should have let me miss that class. But since he didn't, I went up to the teacher, told her that I gave my gymsuit to a poor starving orphan who needed it to trade for a bowl of rice, and sat down to watch another volleyball game.

Afterwards, in the locker room, everybody came over to ask me what had happened. Nancy really knows how to spread news quickly. I just said that Mr. Stone was mad at Ms. Finney and didn't want students to interfere.

It was strange. In Ms. Finney's class we had read *To Kill a Mockingbird* and talked about the part where Atticus tells Jem that you can't understand someone until you've walked around in his or her shoes. So now I tried, in my head, to put myself in Ms. Finney's place, and in Mr. Stone's, and in my father's and mother's. It was horribly confusing. It sure gets tough when you get older. It's much easier to be a little kid whose big problem is learning to tie shoelaces.

Next period, while I was still trying to think, Nancy passed me a note, trying not to let the teacher see it.

Marcy, some of the kids are coming over to my house after school to make plans about how to help Ms Finney. Can you come over? Joel will be there.

Nanci

That's just like Nancy to change the spelling of her name and to dot the i with a big dumb circle. I guess it's a stage people go through, but I'm never going to do it. The dot looks too much like a blimp. When I looked up, I smiled at Nancy, who was pretending to solve an algebra equation.

Finally the bell rang, announcements were made, and I headed for my locker. Joel was standing there.

"How did it go with Mr. Stone?"

I just shook my head.

"He called me in too."

"Did he tell you about his daughter?"

"No. He said that I was a troublemaker and that I was a bad influence on you."

That was amazing. Why did everybody keep trying to team Joel and me up? I mean, we'd just started talking to each other.

I just stood there and blushed. I blush a lot. That's really embarrassing. So, rather than just standing there, I opened my locker. When I did, some of the books fell out. My locker cleanliness would never get *Good Housekeeping*'s Seal of Approval. Joel just laughed and helped me pick up the books.

Then he said, "We'd better hurry up.

Nancy's expecting us, and I want to get there to make sure that things are done."

We walked over to Nancy's house and talked. It was getting easier to talk to him. But I still felt like a blimp. I mean, I was fat. That hadn't changed. Although I had stopped eating a lot of junk, I still hadn't lost much weight.

When we got to Nancy's house, I offered to help her get the food ready. Joel went downstairs, and Nancy and I worked in the kitchen.

"Marcy, how come you never take gym?"

"I don't like volleyball."

"But you never play when we do anything else."

"I'm not coordinated."

"A lot of kids aren't."

"Nancy, I don't want to talk about it."

"But, Marcy, you should. Ms. Finney always said it's better to talk about things that bother you instead of keeping them inside."

I thought about that. Maybe I should tell her. But I was afraid that she would laugh or tell someone.

"Promise not to tell."

"Yeah."

"I hate getting into a gymsuit. I'm too fat and ugly and I hate dressing and undressing and showering in front of everybody."

Then I started to cry.

"Marcy. Come on. You're not ugly. You *are* too fat, but you have good points too. It's just that kids think you're stuck-up because you won't play and because you're smart."

"Do they care?"

"Sure. You can be fun to be with, and you say good things when you're not scared."

"Nancy, are you friends with me just because your mother makes you do that?"

Nancy thought about that and said, "It sort of started out that way, but then I really got to like you."

I didn't know what to say about that, so I said, "I guess we should bring the food downstairs now."

We brought the stuff downstairs. There were a lot of kids there. I sat down next to Joel because he asked me to.

"Marcy, what took you so long?"

"Do you think I'm stuck-up?"

"No. Who told you that? Nancy?"

"Yeah. She said some other kids thought I was."

"People always say that about other people who are quiet, because they are harder to know and more mysterious. But look at you lately. You've been talking a lot."

"That's because you're a bad influence on me. That's what Mr. Stone says, so it must be true."

We both laughed at that. I was proud of myself for that line. For a minute, I almost forgot that I was a blimp.

Nancy passed around cookies, but I refused to have any. She smiled at me when I did that, but didn't make a big deal about it. Then she said that we should all get down to business.

Everyone started making suggestions. The meeting got pretty wild, so rather than trying to explain it, here are the secretary's notes of the meeting:

PROBLEM:

What to do to show everyone how we feel about Ms. Finney and her being fired.

PROBLEM SOLUTIONS:

1. Clog up the faculty-room toilets with *The New York Times* school supplements.

2. Sit in at the Board of Education offices, the front office, and the cafeteria.
3. Demand aspirin from the school nurse.
4. Steal all the chalk in the entire school.
5. Put out an underground newspaper.
6. Put out a contract on Mr. Stone.
7. Short-sheet the beds in the nurse's clinic.
8. Go to the Guidance Counselors and ask for guidance.
9. Boycott the school cafeteria.
10. Capture the intercom system and announce that school has been dismissed.
11. Picket.
12. Steal the faculty-room coffee pot.
13. Put a padlock on the faculty smoking lounge.
14. Circulate petitions showing support of Ms. Finney.
15. Have every kid in the school light up a cigarette at an assigned time, so that the entire student body would get suspended at once.
16. Burn all the copies of the intelligence tests, or make Mr. Stone

take one and announce the results at the next PTA meeting.

17. Plant grass on Mr. Stone, call the cops, and have him busted.
18. Deflate all the volleyballs.
19. Call all the major TV networks and have them cover the story.
20. Try to get our parents to support Ms. Finney.
21. Turn in all our assignments written in crayon.
22. Refuse to leave homeroom until we get a promise that Mr. Stone will listen to us.
23. Cut school and then forge notes saying that we were absent because of cases of acute acne.

Needless to say, we decided not to do most of those things. What we planned to do was get petitions signed, try to get our parents to help, and refuse to leave homeroom until we could talk to Mr. Stone. We thought that if we could organize and get at least ten kids from each homeroom to refuse to leave, we would mess everything up, and then Mr. Stone would have to listen to our representatives. They voted and elected four of us, Joel, Nancy, Robert Alexander, and me. They said that we were the logical choices because Joel and I had nerve enough to talk up in class, and Nancy did some nutty things but had sense, and Robert knew how to speak Mr. Stone's language. Another first for Marcy, the kid who was afraid of being chosen last for gym teams.

Mrs. Sheridan came down to the recreation room and told us that it was time to be heading home for dinner. I said goodbye to Nancy, and she said she'd call me later.

Joel walked me home. We talked about what would happen when our families found out that we were leading what was happening. I said that my father would probably yell and threaten to cut off my allowance and tell me how stupid I was, and then my mother would try to calm him down. After that, I wasn't sure what would happen. Joel said that he thought his father would approve, but even if he didn't he'd still allow Joel to go ahead with it. I asked what his mother would say and he said, "That's a long story. We'll talk about it at Nancy's party, if you can go."

I said, "O.K. I'll ask my parents tonight." Then we were at my door, and I said goodbye and went inside.

Chapter 11

My mother immediately came up and said, "Marcy, did you have a nice day? Who was that young man? Is he the same one who called? Where did you go? What did you do?"

I waited to make sure that she was all done asking questions. Then I answered.

"Yes, I had a nice day. His name is Joel Anderson, and he called last night. I went over to Nancy Sheridan's to talk about school. And Joel asked me to go to a party at Nancy's on Saturday night. Can I go?"

My mother just stood there and beamed.

"Oh, yes, of course, dear. What are you going to wear? Do you know anything about his family? Is his mother in the PTA?"

"I don't know. All I know is that his father is on the Board of Education. And I'll probably wear blue-jeans and a sweat-shirt."

"Oh, Marcy, you can't. We'll have to go out Saturday afternoon and buy a nice new dress. What will everyone be wearing?"

I was so happy that she said yes that I didn't say I didn't care what everyone would be wearing.

"Look, Mom, I have to go do home-work," I said, and headed up to my room.

While I was sitting at my desk, trying to study and thinking about Joel, Stuart walked in.

"Marcy, play with me."

"What do you want to play?"

"Play teacher."

I took out paper and a felt-tip marker and printed the alphabet in large and small letters.

"Here, Stuart, practice your letters." Stuart sat on the floor and went to work. He was really getting good at it. I con-tinued to do my homework.

Mother called us down for dinner. My father had a late business meeting, so it was just Mom, Stuart, and me. We laughed a lot. It was really fun.

After dinner, Stuart and I went upstairs and I read to him. In the middle of a story, Stuart asked, "Who's Finney?"

"Do you mean Ms. Finney?"

"Yeah. Mommy and Daddy fight about her."

"Oh, Stuart, she's this really great teacher. She talks about good things, like feelings and people and good books and lots of stuff you should like."

"Will she be my teacher when I grow up?"

I thought about that and sighed. "I don't know. I really hope so. I don't know anything anymore."

Then I kissed him good night and watched him shuffle out with Wolf, leaving a trail of orange pits.

Once in bed, I immediately fell asleep and had very strange dreams about my being caught in a bowl of jello.

When I got up in the morning, I dressed quickly and ran down to breakfast. The rest of the family was already there.

My father said, "I hear that you are going to a little party Saturday night with a young man. I'm not sure that I like the fact that my little girl is growing up, but I suppose that I've got to get used to it."

Then he smiled. I smiled back. He continued, stirring his coffee very slowly.

"His father is a radical on the school board. Goes for busing and progressive education. I don't want my daughter involved. You understand, don't you?"

My cornflakes got caught in my throat.

"You know, Marcy, I really don't understand you anymore. You used to be such a good child. Now I just don't know you."

My mother interrupted, "Martin, please don't start. Marcy is a good child. She's just going out. All the girls do at her age. Why, lots of them have been going out for much longer. And I'm sure that Joel is a nice boy."

I just sat there.

Stuart smiled at me across the table. I really loved the weird little kid at that moment. I smiled back and said, "Stuart, tonight I'll read you and Wolf another story."

My father just grunted and said, "That kid and his teddy bear! Stuart, you'd better start growing up."

First he complains that I'm growing up too fast and then he complains that Stuart isn't growing up fast enough.

I asked to be excused, and got my books and went to school. Joel met me outside the building. It felt really good seeing him. A bunch of kids, the same ones who had been at Nancy's, gathered and we made plans. All of us were supposed to spend the day rounding up anyone who would be willing to remain in homeroom after the bell rang. The plan was to organize and be prepared to do it the next day. We settled things pretty quickly, and the day went on.

It was a strange day. Everyone was walking around very quietly. Even while passing between classes, it was almost too silent. People walked around whispering, trying to figure out who was in on it and who wasn't. Nancy, Robert, Joel, and I knew, because we were given the lists, but no one else was positive.

Then it happened. We were sitting in English class, still diagramming sentences, when the room phone buzzed. The sub went to it, and stared around the room while she was listening. She kept shaking her head, and then said, "All right. I'll send them right down."

Then she put down the phone, paused, and said, "Robert Alexander, Joel Anderson, Marcy Lewis, and Nancy Sheridan are wanted in the principal's office immediately. Take your books with you. I don't think you'll be coming back here today."

Everyone turned and looked around. Then all of a sudden someone said, "Uh oh, you guys are gonna get it." The four of us got up, grabbed our books, and left the room. The sub closed the door after us.

We all stood outside the door to the classroom. "What now?" Nancy asked.

"Maybe Stone wants us to audition for the talent show" was Robert's answer. "Perhaps my fame as a harmonica player has spread."

Nancy laughed and said, "I can always do my imitation of an electric toothbrush."

Joel said that he could play his guitar, and I started to tap dance. All the money my parents had put into my lessons finally paid off. We all stood there laughing.

Then I said, "Listen, I'm really scared."

Nancy looked down and said, "Me too."

Joel said, "We're all scared, but we've got to go . . . unless we all plan to run off to Alaska, and that doesn't seem too sensible. We knew what we were getting into, so let's go through with it. At least we'll get our chance to talk to Stone."

We got to the office and went to the front desk. The secretary had the look on her face that she always had whenever a kid was going to get it. I bet when she was a kid she always told on others.

We filed into Mr. Stone's office. It was filled. My mother was there. So was Nancy's. And there was another woman and a man that I didn't know. I glanced to my right and saw Stuart sitting there, clutching Wolf and sucking his thumb.

Mr. Stone said, "I have called your parents here to discuss your plot to undermine my school."

We all stood there. Then Joel said, "There has been no plot to undermine your school. We just want to make ourselves heard in *our* school."

Then the man who was with the women said, "See here, Mr. Stone. I'm not sure what you're trying to accomplish. I've already told you that I trust my son and approve of him."

I looked at Joel, and he nodded his head. "Dad, I would like to introduce Marcy Lewis, Nancy Sheridan, and Robert Alexander —"

Mr. Stone interrupted, "Look, there is a time and a place for everything. I have called all of you together to discuss the student rebellion of which you four are the leaders. What I want from you are the names of all of the students who are involved in this plot, or you four will be in serious trouble."

I said, "Oh, no. That's not fair. No way."

Mr. Stone turned to my mother. "I told you, Mrs. Lewis. See what she has turned into."

My mother looked at him and said, "My

daughter has turned into someone I'm very proud of, and I'm not sure that she is doing anything wrong. I don't appreciate your threatening her."

All of the parents started talking at once. So did we. Everything got noisy and very confused.

The phone rang. Everyone shut up. Mr. Stone picked up the receiver. He listened for a while and then said, "Thank you. That solves a lot of my problems."

Then he got up and started walking around. That was sort of hard. There were so many people in such a small place. But I guess Mr. Stone thought he would win the "Principal of the Year Award" for his performance.

Anyway, he turned and said, "Your plan has no way of working. The Superintendent's Office has ordered school to be closed until the Tuesday hearing."

Then he walked back to his desk. On his way he accidentally knocked over Wolf. Orange pits fell all over the rug, and Stuart started to cry. My mother ran over to Stuart, and so did I. All of a sudden, everybody in the room started to laugh, except for Stuart and Mr. Stone, who turned around and said, "For everyone's information, these four student ringleaders are suspended for ten days. It will go on their permanent records, and they will not be allowed to make up work missed. You might as well take them home. I don't want them on school grounds for the entire time that they are suspended."

We all walked out of the office and into the hall. I heard my mother inviting everyone over to our house to discuss the situation. Then she, Stuart, and I went to my locker to get my coat and books.

I said, "Thanks, Mom. I'm sorry to get you involved in this."

"Marcy, do you believe in what you're doing?"

"Yes, I do."

"Then I'm very proud of you. I wish I had nerve enough to do it. But I'm scared. What is your father going to say?"

"Mom, I've spent thirteen years worrying about that, and I've never been happy. So now I've got to do things that I think are right."

Then I closed my locker and we walked out to the car.

"Honey, don't think I'm mad at you, but shouldn't you clean out your locker? People will think that I never taught you to be neat."

I just looked at her and laughed. That's

just like my mother — in the middle of everything, she worries about my locker. But she certainly had surprised me. She was on my side.

On the way home, I asked, "Mom, how come all of you came to school?"

My mother explained. "I got a call from Mr. Stone's office. Naturally, I had to bring Stuart with me. When I got to school, I ran into Nancy's mother and the other parents. Mr. Stone called us into the office, told us how bad you all were, and how we should support him, especially me, because of the PTA. Mr. Anderson told him that he was proud of Joel and would personally congratulate his son, not punish him. The only one who went along with Mr. Stone was Mrs. Alexander, who cried the whole time. Then he called you in, and you know the rest of the story. Oh, Marcy, what are we going to tell your father?"

"Mom, I don't know. He's gonna yell a lot, but I don't know what to do."

Stuart sat in the middle and kept pretending to drive. Poor kid. He's in the middle most of the time.

Getting to our house, we rushed inside to get ready for everybody else.

"Mom, how do you think Mr. Stone found out who the leaders are?"

"He said that a student told him."

"What a rat."

"Marcy, you shouldn't talk about Mr. Stone that way."

"I meant the kid, but Stone's a rat, too."

"Marcy!" But then she laughed.

"Mom, Stone says Ms. Finney never taught us anything, but I know that 'Stone's a rat' is a metaphor. I bet he doesn't know that."

"Marcy, stop fooling around. We have company coming."

The bell rang. Everybody came in. We all sat around for a few minutes, getting food and staring at one another.

Mr. Anderson started. "I'm very proud of our children. Although I think their scheme was drastic, I feel that Mr. Stone has treated them as mindless children, and they've proved him wrong. They know what they want and are willing to accept the consequences. I think they've learned a very important lesson."

Mrs. Alexander just kept crying.

My mother said, "This won't keep our children out of college, will it? We do want Marcy to get a good education."

Mr. Anderson put down his coffee cup and lit up a cigarette. "Listen, don't let Mr. Stone intimidate you. We have bright children, and many schools will respect their minds and their initiative."

Robert, Nancy, Joel, and I sat on the floor watching the whole scene. Finally Nancy said, "Look. We made the decision to support Ms. Finney, and I'm glad. I'll use the suspension time to study."

"Yeah," I said. "We can get the assignments and do them anyway."

"But we won't get credit for it. Why bother?" Robert asked.

Joel said, "We can use the time to learn something, instead of diagramming sentences."

We all laughed.

"I think you should go to the library and get some books out concerning legal rights and privileges," Joel's father suggested. "You can learn some interesting things. This situation can turn into a real learning experience for you."

Finally Mrs. Alexander spoke up. "I don't know about the rest of you, but my Robert will be punished. I don't agree with the stand he is taking or your attitude about it. Come, Robert, we're going home." She got out of her chair and turned to leave. "Robert, I told you that we are leaving. Now, let's go."

Robert got up. He looked upset and

mad. I didn't blame him. I knew what he was going through.

They left. The rest of us talked about the upcoming hearing. No one was sure that Ms. Finney would win. Mr. Anderson said that he was in a funny position, being a school-board member and everything. He had a feeling that Mr. Stone would try to get him disqualified.

My mother offered to contact those members of the PTA who might help.

Mrs. Sheridan offered to work with her.

Mr. Anderson said that he would help, but it would have to be during evenings.

My mother said, "Perhaps Joel's mother would like to help during the day."

Joel looked uncomfortable. His father smiled and said, "My wife and I are divorced. She doesn't live around here."

I jumped up. "Does anyone want Coke or coffee or anything?"

They all said no and that it was time to go home for dinner. I said good-bye to Mrs. Sheridan, Nancy, Mr. Anderson, and Joel.

After they left, I turned to my mother. "Why did you have to do that?"

"Do what?"

"Ask them about the mother. If they wanted to say anything, they would have."

My mother looked surprised, "Oh, I'm sorry. I didn't realize. Do you think they think I'm horrible?"

"I don't know. I doubt it. But please don't do it again, Mom. I'm happy that you're helping me with this school thing." I hugged her.

"I did a lot of thinking," she said. "I'm very proud of you. I never could have done that when I was your age. So now, at my age, I'm learning and you're my teacher. The world is changing . . . and I'm glad."

I hugged her again. Sometimes it's very hard to say anything.

"Joel is very nice, Marcy. Do you like him? Does he like you?"

"I don't know, Mom. Yeah, I like him. But it's no big romance. Don't bug me about it. I think he just thinks I'm a good friend. We like some of the same things."

Stuart walked in and asked for an orange. We both ate one and spent the rest of the afternoon stuffing orange pits in Wolf's head. Actually, we turned it into a game, putting Wolf in a corner and trying to pitch the pits into the hole. I won, 84 to 39. It took almost all afternoon to get that score.

I heard the car door slam and the front door open. The ritual had begun. Only this time it was a little different. This time he called me downstairs before he was even handed his drink.

I walked in and said, "Hi. How was your day?"

"Apparently not as exciting as yours, young lady. I warned you about getting involved. Maybe it's about time that you got punished for your actions. I had to hear all about this from a business associate. I understand that both of my girls are involved in this? Is that true?"

My mother said, "Let's all sit down and discuss this quietly."

So we all sat down. I looked from one to the other. Then I said, "I'm doing the right thing. I'm not always wrong."

"Martin, Marcy's right. You should've heard Mr. Stone."

He just sat there, chewing on his smelly cigar. My mother continued, "She's got to make her own decisions. And I've made my own decision too. I'm going to support and help her. She's helped me to realize some things."

My father turned on me. "Are you satisfied now? Your mother and I never disagree."

"Don't blame her," Mom said. "I've made up my own mind."

"Can I please be excused?"

"Oh, no you don't, young lady. You cause all the trouble and then you try to slip away."

"Martin!"

"Oh, all right. Marcy, I want you to go to bed without your dinner. You may leave."

I went up to my room, closed the door, and looked in the mirror and searched for emerging acne. There was none. So I sat down at my desk. Then I realized that I didn't have anything to do. I'd been suspended. Me, of all people. So I spent the next hour thinking of Joel.

Joel was a special person, I decided. He was smart. He was brave. He was cute. And he liked me. Amazing.

I stayed in my room all evening and watched television. TV comes in handy when people can't talk to each other. Then I went to bed and dreamed about going to Nancy's party and falling down a flight of stairs.

Chapter 12

The next morning my mother came into my room and woke me up.

"Marcy. I let you sleep late today, but it's time to get up. We're going shopping for your dress. And I want to talk to you."

I hate waking up out of a sound sleep. She expects me to talk and make sense immediately. So I rolled over on my stomach and put the pillow over my head. She started to tickle me. I hate that too.

It was easier to get out of bed than to be tickled. My mother thinks she's being cute when she does that. I think she's being a pain.

"Mom, what do you want?"

"I'm getting nervous about what's going on. I don't like to fight with your father. I'm not used to it."

I flopped down on the bed and put the

pillow back on my head. I could feel her sit down on the edge of the bed. I tightened up, expecting to be tickled again. When that didn't happen, I peeked out from under the pillow. I could see her crying.

Sitting up, I reached over, and touched her hair. "Aw, Mom, please don't cry. It'll be O.K. I'm sorry."

"Marcy, it's not your fault. It's not anybody's fault. It just happened. I never really thought much about women's liberation. Now I'm beginning to."

"Look, Mom, let's go shopping. Don't worry."

So we went shopping, taking Stuart and Wolf with us.

I hate to go shopping. I love clothes, but they always look awful on me. All those skinny tops, and the clothes that expect you to have a waist. And when you find something you like, they never have it in your size. It's horrible. One of the worst things is that I have to go into the store, go past the junior boutique, and step into the "Chubbies" section. They should give out paper bags to wear over your head while you shop there.

So there we were at the "Chubbies" section. Stuart was swinging on one of the coat racks. My mother was looking at ugly dresses. I was trying to avoid the saleslady.

She waddled up to my mother. She was what the store people would call a "stylish stout." She was what I would call a "senior blimp."

"Can I help you, dearie?" she asked.

"We are looking for a party dress for my daughter."

"Oh, isn't she sweet. What do you want, honey?" she asked me.

"I want a pair of size five bluejeans."

"Marcy," my mother began.

"Mom, she asked what I wanted, not what I was going to get."

"You'll have to excuse my daughter. She gets upset when she shops."

The lady smiled and said, "I can understand. I used to be that way myself."

I felt like throwing up when she said that.

My mother must have understood, because she said, "Perhaps it would be best if we browsed by ourselves. We'll be sure to call you if we need help. Thank you." My mother's O.K. sometimes, even if she is skinny.

We took lots of stuff into the dressing room. Finally, I found a purple pants suit that I liked. My mother liked it, even if it wasn't a dress. I guess she gave in because she was getting tired of pulling Stuart out from under racks, and of searching for the perfect outfit that was going to turn me into an all-American princess.

Then we went to the jewelry department. That's fun. It doesn't matter what size you are when you buy a necklace. I bought a pair of hoop earrings, a necklace, and a ring. I felt really good. And it was nice to see my mother happy. Even Stuart was happy. My mother bought him a pair of sneakers, and the salesman gave him a balloon.

In the afternoon I went over to Nancy's house. She's going out with a tenth-grader at Hoover High School. Nancy's been going out since seventh grade, and she knows lots more about guys than I do.

"Nancy, do you think Joel likes me?"

"He asked you out, didn't he?"

"Yeah. But I don't know why."

"Oh, Marcy, come on. You're not so bad."

"Yeah. But he's so nice."

"So are you. Listen, Marcy, Joel's a great guy, a little too serious sometimes, but nice. I don't think he goes out much, though. So if he asked you out, he must like you."

"Really think so?"

"Yeah, I don't think he's the kind to fall madly in love, but I think you and he can be friends."

"You don't think he can fall in love?"

"Marcy, you're weird. First you're afraid that he doesn't like you and then you wonder whether he can fall in love."

I blushed. Can I help it if I get confused easily?

I told Nancy that I was nervous because everyone was going to be dancing and all I knew was tap and ballet, and that wasn't "in" at parties. So Nancy and I practiced all afternoon.

When I got home, I practiced all the dance steps in front of the mirror. My mother walked in and tried to do them too. Sometimes I wish she'd act her age.

Dinner went pretty well. My father seemed happy because we had bought clothes.

"See," he said, hugging my mother. "My family can get nice things because I work so hard."

The phone rang. My father answered it and called out, "Marcy, it's your Romeo." I was so embarrassed that I didn't want to go to the phone. But I had to.

"Hi."

"Hi, Juliet."

"Oh, Joel, I'm sorry. My father thinks he's funny."

"I'll live. So will you. What did you do today?"

"Some shopping . . . and then I saw Nancy."

"I talked to some of the kids today. It's hard to get everything together now that school's cancelled. Listen. Tomorrow, I'll pick you up at 8. O.K.?"

"Sure."

"Good. Well, listen, I'll see you later."

"O.K. Bye."

As I put down the receiver, I looked up and saw my father.

"Hi, Dad."

"Marcy, we never talk anymore. Let's talk now."

"Daddy. I have to practice my dancing."

"This will only take a few minutes."

So we sat down in the living room and he started. I could tell that he was going to try to stay calm. And he did try. He hardly raised his voice. It sounded as if he'd rehearsed it.

He said, "I realize you're growing up and have to start making your own decisions. But I don't approve of you not saying the Pledge. And I don't think you should support Miss Finney."

"*Ms.* Finney," I said.

"All right, *Ms.* Finney, if you insist."

I stopped chewing my nails long enough to explain to him that while I did support Ms. Finney, I still said the Pledge.

He said that he hadn't realized that. Still, he disagreed with my support of Ms. Finney.

"You've got to learn to stick with the majority, to play the game. And Marcy, now that you are going out, I want you to remember to be a good girl. You must protect your good name."

I laughed. He sat there, looking uncomfortable and chewing on his cigar.

"Dad, I promise not to elope before I'm sixteen, bring home another mouth to feed, join a motorcycle gang, or mug little old ladies."

He raised his voice a little. "Stop acting like a smart aleck. Can't you understand? I just want my family to be happy."

I said, "O.K., but don't worry about me." Then he said, "I'm glad we've talked." Then he shook my hand. He shook my hand. A hug would have been nicer, but that was better than nothing, and he hadn't yelled too loud.

My mother walked in. "How would you both like some ice cream?"

"No thanks, Mom. I'm going to go upstairs." I spent the rest of the evening washing my face with special anti-acne soap, brushing my hair, and looking in the mirror to see if giving up the bowl of ice cream had made me skinny.

Chapter 13

The next day, I had to babysit. My parents were going shopping and I had to take care of Stuart and his bear. Sometimes I feel that my parents should claim Wolf on their income tax.

I took him over to the playground, swung him for a while, and then ran him around on the merry-go-round until we both got dizzy. Wolf, of course, never gets dizzy. According to Stuart, that's because he's so healthy from the orange pits.

We sat down on a bench.

"Stuart, are you happy?"

"What?"

"Are you happy?"

He nodded his head up and down.

"Why?"

"I love you."

I hugged him. "Are you always happy?"

He just looked at me.

"Stuart, do you think you're happy because you're just a little kid and don't know any better?"

No answer yet.

I could see that my question wasn't going to get answered. What can you expect from a four-year-old, the wisdom of Moses?

"Stuart, do you love Wolf?"

"Yes."

"Mommy?"

"Yes."

"Daddy?"

"Yes."

"What makes you cry?"

"When I fall down."

"What else?"

"When you cry."

"Anything else?"

"When Daddy yells."

"Do you love Daddy?"

"Yes."

Sometimes I wish I were four years old.

"Marcy."

"Yes."

"I'm hungry."

So I took him home and made him a peanut butter and ham sandwich. That's what he wanted, and I figured that since it was so easy to make him happy, I should do it. He'll learn soon enough what sad is. He'd just finished it when we heard the car drive up.

"It's Mommy and Daddy," he yelled.

Rushing outside, he grabbed hold of my mother's legs and said, "I miss you."

Nice. The kid doesn't cry or anything all day and then he acts like it wasn't any good.

"What did you get me?"

Great. He sometimes thinks the whole word is like a quiz show.

My mother laughed and said, "Come inside. I'll show you."

Everyone came in. Stuart. My mother. And my father.

"Hi, honey. How did it go?"

"Fine, Mom. We went to the playground."

She picked out two bags. "One for Stuart and one for you."

We ripped open the bags. Stuart got a pair of mittens, and I got a floppy hat.

"Oh, Mom, I love it."

"The saleslady said all the girls are wearing them, and it'll draw attention to your face."

All of a sudden I felt horrible. Why did she always worry about what everybody else is wearing, and why'd she have to remind me that I have to do stuff to draw attention from the neck up because the rest of me is so glunky?

My father looked at me and said, "Don't you start getting oversensitive, young lady. Your mother wanted to make you happy. Now be happy."

I had to laugh.

We all started to laugh. Stuart had taken the hat and put it on Wolf.

Then we put the packages away, and Mom and I started making dinner. Stuart, Wolf, and Dad headed for the TV.

"Marcy, I bought the hat for you because I liked it and thought you would like it. Do I always talk about how everybody else dresses?"

"Yeah, you do. Ms. Finney says that clothes can be an artistic expression of the individual. Mom, I don't want to look like everybody else, even if I could."

"I'm sorry. It's just that it's safer being like every one else."

"Mom, are you happy?"

"What do you mean?"

"Are you happy?"

"I don't think about that much. I'm happy when you are happy. You are very important to me."

"Do you love Daddy?"

"Yes, Marcy, I do. I don't always agree with him, but he's very good to me."

"He's not very good to me."

"Please. Don't say that. Daddy loves you very much. He just doesn't know how to show it."

"I bet he wishes that I'd never been born. Right?" I ask.

"No, of course not. What a silly question. You're our daughter and we both really love you."

I finished setting the table, and we all sat down to eat. All of a sudden it dawned on me that it really was the night of Nancy's party. It was my very first date. I was kind of calm and frightened to death at the same time.

Once dinner was over, I rushed upstairs to get ready. I spent fifteen minutes brushing my teeth and another ten searching for pimples. I thought that I found one and then realized that it was a blot from my felt-tip pen. An orange pimple would have been a little strange, even for me. So I washed my face.

Getting dressed was a real trip. I got nervous about the color of the outfit. Purple was a pretty color, but what if I looked like a large grape in it? I was sure that everyone at the party was going to say "Joel, who is that grape you're dragging around?" Or "Marcy, Halloween is over." When I put on the earrings, necklace, and ring, I felt better. I mean, grapes don't wear jewelry. People would know it was me.

My mother came into the room. She started gushing about how nice I looked, how I was growing up, and how my clothes did express my personality.

The doorbell rang. My mother wanted me to wait a while to make an entrance. I rushed down the steps, trying to get to the front door before my father got there.

I didn't make it. My father and Joel were standing there looking at each other. I walked over and said, "Hi. I'll get my coat and we can leave."

But it wasn't that easy. My mother came down the steps, making the entrance that I didn't make, and said, "Well, hello, Joel. Why don't we all go sit in the living room and talk for a while?"

I thought I would die right there. But I didn't, so we all went into the living room. It was horrible. My father kept chomping on his smelly cigar and asking Joel what his plans for the future were. My mother kept gushing about how nice I looked. Stuart wandered in and asked Joel if he was going to marry me. Joel just sat there, smiling and trying to say nice things.

I couldn't say anything. I just sat there, trying not to have a nervous breakdown and wishing that a tornado would strike or that some machine would come out of the sky to rescue us. I was positive that I was developing an ulcer.

Finally I stood up and said, "We'd better go. Nancy's expecting me to help her out."

So everybody stood up and walked over to the door. I felt as if we were leaving for a trip to Mars. All we needed were reporters around, asking questions like "Ms. Lewis, how does it feel to be going out on your first date?" and "Mr. Anderson, has it been a life-long ambition of yours to go out with a grape?" My father told us to get home early, and my mother kept picking imaginary lint off my coat.

We finally got out the door and started down the street. Then I looked at Joel to tell him how sorry I was about the scene at the house. Instead, we both laughed.

Chapter 14

By the time we got to Nancy's house, my stomach had calmed down. Ringing the bell, we heard someone running up to the door. It was Nancy, looking absolutely beautiful in a long skirt and a short top. On me it would have looked like a lot of rubber bands above a tent placed on a volleyball.

Standing behind Nancy was this fantastic-looking guy, the kind you always see in ads for aftershave lotion. I had never been that near to anyone who looked like him. Nancy introduced us. It was her boyfriend, Phil. I'd seen him around but had never talked to him. He smiled and said, "Nancy's been telling me what's happening. Wish we had as much excitement at that stupid high school. Maybe it'll get more interesting next year, when you get there."

Joel said, "Why don't all of you at the high school get involved? It's something that could happen there too."

Phil and Joel got really involved in the discussion, and so did Nancy and I. We finally headed down to the rec room, all of us carrying plates of food. The place was mobbed.

Some of the kids were dancing. I kept trying to remember all the things Nancy had taught me. Then Joel turned to me, saying, "Listen, Marcy. I'm a lousy dancer. So let's go talk."

We went over to a couch and sat down. Everyone was either dancing or standing around eating food. I didn't know how to begin talking. I'd talked to him before, but somehow this was different. And he wasn't saying anything either. So I sat there, looking at the dancers and smiling as if I were having a fantastic time.

All of a sudden, a pretzel flew across the room and hit the wall right behind us. We looked around the room.

It was Andy Moore. He's always getting sent to the principal's office because he shoots straw wrappers at everyone in the cafeteria. He waved at us, and we waved back.

Joel began, "That Andy is really dumb.

He'll do anything for attention."

I said, "Ms. Finney says that we've got to try to understand people, maybe not like them, but try to understand."

He thought for a minute. "Yeah. I guess so, but sometimes it's hard. I wish Ms. Finney was still around."

"So do I. Nancy's mother ran into her at the grocery story. She said Ms. Finney's going to fight."

He stared ahead, and then looked down at his hands. "I'm glad. She's one of the few people I can talk to. It's kind of hard. My father's a neat guy and I can talk to him. But my grandmother doesn't understand much, and she lives with us."

"Where's your mother?"

"My parents are divorced. She lives in Denver. She's remarried. I don't like her."

It seemed hard for Joel to talk about it, so I didn't ask any questions.

But he continued, "My dad's a lawyer. Gets involved in a lot of controversial cases. He gave up corporate law to start his own practice. My mother got upset and said that he should stay where the money was and not always be defending weirdos. But they're not all weirdos. Some are poor and need help. He's really a good guy."

"So she moved?"

"Yeah. She likes things to be easy. And she didn't like a lot of my father's friends . . . too radical, she said. So one day she decided to divorce my father. She wanted to take me with her, but I didn't want to go. She cried a lot and said she'd go to court to get me, but I told her that I hated her and refused to go."

"What did she say?"

"She said that she'd let me stay with Dad until she got resettled and then send for me."

"Oh, Joel, when's that going to happen," I said, feeling panic. What if Joel had to move away? Joel and Ms. Finney gone. I couldn't stand it.

"It won't. One day we got a letter saying that she was getting married to a school principal. I had to go out to Denver to visit her. That's where she's teaching and where she met him. He's just like Mr. Stone. I can't believe there are two of them. Anyway, I went out there and was so bad that the principal didn't want me, and she went along with him. I hate her. I really do. I'm glad she gave up after a while."

"Does it bother you?"

"No . . . yeah, I guess it does. Maybe that's why I don't trust that many people."

"You can trust me."

"I know that you're O.K., but I just want you to know that I'm not the type to go out much or get hung up on anybody."

"O.K."

"Marcy, let's be friends."

"O.K."

I felt very strange. There was a lot to think about . . . Joel being bad . . . his mother leaving . . . a stepfather like Mr. Stone . . . Joel not wanting to get serious but still wanting a friend . . . my own feelings about Joel.

Nancy and Phil picked that moment to come over and talk.

"Hey, having fun? Why aren't you dancing?" Nancy asked.

"I don't," Joel answered.

"But Marcy spent all week learning."

I could have killed her.

Joel turned to me and said, "Sorry about that," and we both laughed.

"That's O.K. The lessons might come in handy some day," I said.

Robert Alexander came over.

"Hi. Thought your mother wouldn't let you come, " Joel said.

"That dope. She's driving me crazy. I snuck out."

"What'll happen if she finds out?"

"She won't . . . Even if she does, I don't

care. She said I have to go to boarding school. I hate her."

Phil held up a six-pack and said, "Anybody want a beer?"

Joel, Robert, and Nancy took cans, so I did. I opened my can and took a sip. I'd tasted beer before and thought it was horrible. It still was.

I asked Nancy where her parents were. I was kind of nervous about the beer.

"They went to a movie. I told them I was old enough to not have chaperones. So they gave in. They're cool."

I just nodded my head, then pretended to sip my beer. A cream soda would have been better. We all sat around talking.

At one end of the room there was a lot of noise. Andy Moore was putting beer cans on their sides and karate-chopping them. I asked Nancy if her parents were going to be mad because of the beer.

"Listen," she said. "They're so glad I don't smoke dope that they think beer's O.K."

So I just stood there, watching and pretending to drink. Everybody else was dancing or chug-a-lugging. Joel turned to me and said, "Listen, Marcy. Let's go. This party is going to get out of hand. I'd rather just talk."

Waving to Nancy, we left. Joel and I walked back to my house.

"Joel, do you like beer?"

"Yeah. Why?"

"Just wondered."

"Don't you?"

"No."

"Then why did you drink it?"

"Everyone was."

"Marcy, you don't have to drink just because everyone does. Look, you're different. That's cool."

I thought, Yeah, really cool. I don't look like everyone else. I don't take gym like everyone else. And sometimes I don't feel like everyone else.

Instead I said, "I don't want to be different."

Joel stopped and looked at me. "Ms. Finney's different. Do you think she wants to be like everyone else?"

That was hard. Ms. Finney was special, very special. Some people can be different and still be happy. I personally think that while blimps are different, they are not special and not happy.

We continued walking. I didn't know what to say. I guess Joel must have realized how down I was.

"Remember the time Robert told Ms.

Finney how he cried while watching *Gone With the Wind* and she said she hadn't realized how sentimental he was and he said, 'Yeah, someone stole my popcorn'?"

We laughed.

Then I said, "What about the time she invited her friend in and they both played guitars and talked about poetry and music?"

"And all the old movies she brought in."

"And the word games."

"And how she let us videotape our play."

"And the time she had us do the Blind Walk and blindfolded one person and had one lead the other around."

"That was neat. It was a good beginning to *The Miracle Worker*."

"I miss her."

"Me, too."

By that time we'd reached the front door to my house. I was really happy thinking about all the good times with Ms. Finney.

We stood at the door. All of a sudden, I got scared. What if Joel wanted to kiss me good night? I'd never kissed anyone before, except relatives, and they didn't count. I mean, kissing Stuart on the forehead to "make it all better" isn't exactly thrilling. And practicing and pretending with a pillow isn't the same as the real thing, either. What if I turned out to be a lousy kisser? Even worse, what if Joel didn't even want to kiss me? Either way, it was going to be pretty hard to deal with.

I opened my purse and started to look for my keys. My purse always has so much junk in it that it takes forever to find anything. I dropped half the stuff on the ground, and then we had to search for everything. I found my keys and just stood there.

"I guess I should go inside now. Thanks for a nice time." It was dumb, but I couldn't think of anything else to say.

Joel leaned over. He was actually going to kiss me. I closed my eyes like they always do in the movies and on TV. I felt a quick kiss on my forehead. It was the type of kiss I get when my mother tucks me in. So much for my career as a sex fiend.

A light went on in the living room, so I said, "I'd better go in now."

We said good night. When I got inside, my mother was waiting.

"Did you have a nice time, dear?"

"Yeah."

"Did everyone like your new clothes — oh, I'm sorry. I forgot. Do you think Joel will ask you out again?"

I shrugged my shoulders.

"Why don't you know? Did something go wrong?"

"Mom, please don't start. I had a good time."

She looked at me and said, "I only want you to be happy, Marcy. I don't want you to be miserable the way I was when I was little."

I didn't know what to say to her. So I hugged her and went to bed. Then I lay awake, trying to figure everything out and wondering whether I'd wake up with pimples all over my face.

Chapter 15

My phone rang and woke me up the next morning. It was Nancy, in a bad mood. The kids had helped her clean up after the party, but when her parents came home they found a couple of the guys in the back yard, throwing up. In the future, they said, they would stay home when she had parties.

I thought she got off easy. If it had been my family, my mother would be in hysterics and my father would be screaming for blood.

Nancy asked if I wanted to come over and listen to some records. I really wanted to but had to go see my grandmother, so I told her that I'd call when we got back.

When I got downstairs, I saw that the Sunday paper had been delivered. I picked up the funny sheets, and my father took them away. He said that since he paid for the paper, he had the right to read it first. Then he put them beside his chair and read the sports section.

I got mad. I screamed, "I hate you! You're a real creep," and ran up to my room and slammed the door and locked it.

It all happened before I realized that I was going to do it. I was scared. I didn't know what was going to happen next.

I could hear him yelling. He was telling my mother and Stuart how bad and ungrateful I was, how hard he worked and all he wanted was peace and quiet and how I never let him have any. Finally he shut up, and then I heard my mother coming up the steps.

She came to my room and tried to open the door. Then she knocked. I sat on my bed and screamed, "Leave me alone! Can't everyone in this dumb family just leave me alone?"

She knocked again and said, "Marcy, please let me in, or else I'll have to tell your father." So I let her in.

"Marcy, don't be mad at me. It's not my fault."

I threw myself back on the bed and put the pillow over my head.

She started to cry. This time I didn't even care. Then I heard my father's voice.

"See what you've done, young lady. You've made your mother cry. Apologize or you won't be able to go out on any more dates."

My head was still under the pillow. I wanted to stay there and smother, but I sat up and said, "Leave me alone. Just leave me alone. I hate you."

My father raised his hand. He had never hit me before, but this time it looked as if I was going to get clobbered.

My mother grabbed his arm and screamed, "Martin! Please don't. Nobody made me cry. I did it myself. Don't hit her."

He looked at both of us. She was trying to stop crying. I was staring at him. He glared at me and said, "Get that snarl off your face. You look like an animal." Then he turned and left, slamming the door.

My mother was still standing there. I wanted to be alone, so I went back under the pillow. I heard her leave. My head ached. It was hard to breathe. I just wanted to be dead.

Someone tapped me on the back. I peeked out. It was Stuart.

"What do you want?"

He patted me on the head and said, "I love you. Give me a kiss."

So I kissed and held him. Poor little kid. It's scary when something like this happens.

My mother came back in and said, "We'd all better get ready. Your father wants to leave in half an hour."

So we went. The visit to my grandmother was horrible. Everyone was in a rotten mood. My father kept telling her what a monster I was.

Sometimes I feel guilty hating him, but he deserves it.

Chapter 16

Joel called the next day. His grandmother was making him buy a birthday present to send to his mother. He didn't want to get one, but figured that it was easier than fighting.

I rushed downstairs to tell my mother that I'd be going out. She got upset because I was wearing bluejeans and a sweatshirt. She said that even though I was "plump," I didn't have to look like a slob.

I told her that I wasn't going to change, that until I saw her I had been happy with the way I looked, and that if her advice meant that I was going to end up with a guy like my father, I didn't want to bother.

She got really mad then, and told me that I was becoming an unmanageable brat.

I walked out of the house and sat on the front steps, waiting for Joel. My mother came out and said that she couldn't take any more fighting.

"Mom, I don't want to fight with you either. But you can't tell me what to do all the time. I'm not a baby."

"I know, but a child is always her mother's baby."

That seemed silly. Did that mean that my father was still my grandmother's baby, or that Mr. Stone was someone's baby? I doubted that Joel was his mother's baby. I bet Ms. Finney's mother didn't think she was a baby.

"Marcy, you're so important to me. I don't have anyone else to talk to."

"Mom, what about Mrs. Sheridan? Talk to her."

"Oh, I can't. There are certain things that you keep in the family."

"Well, tell Stuart. I can't stand it. You tell me things, and then when I tell you I hate my father, you get upset. What do you want from me?"

"Try to understand. I'm trying to change and grow. Marcy, it's not easy for me. I know it's not easy for you either. Let's try to help each other."

"Why'd you marry him?"

"If I hadn't, you and Stuart wouldn't be here."

"Yeah, I know . . . but that's not why you married him . . . is it? Uh . . . Mom, did you have to get married?"

"Marcy! Your father and I were married for two years before you were born. You know that. I married your father because I loved him. I still do. We need each other. Don't you understand?"

I shrugged my shoulders. Why couldn't she understand? I mean, I'm just a kid. Why couldn't she talk to Mrs. Sheridan or someone? Why me?

Joel was coming down the block. He waved, and I waved back. My mother looked and then said, "I guess that's it. You want to be with Joel, not me. Have a nice time," she said, walking into the house.

Joel walked up to the steps.

"Hi."

"Hi. Ready?"

"Yeah."

"Did you and your mother just have a fight?"

"Well, not really a fight. A discussion."

"Was it O.K.?"

"Oh, Joel, who knows? Let's go."

So we took off, and ended up going to a

shopping plaza, one of those places that has every kind of store. All the kids hang out there, so we ran into a lot of people. But we had to go look for a dumb present for Joel's mother.

He was in a weird mood, laughing a lot but also a little angry. At first I thought I'd done something wrong, but Joel said, "No, I'm just mad 'cause I have to get something for my mother."

It was funny. He kept looking in all of the stores, trying to decide what to get. He looked at an anthill farm, a plaque that said "God Bless Our Happy Home," a rock record, a Monopoly game, a green shade of nail polish, and a button that said, "Kiss me. I'm neurotic." Finally he picked out a really ugly heart-shaped pin with red, green, and orange rhinestones. It was atrocious.

We found it in one of those horrible stores that sell lots of junk: striped purple and yellow toilet seats, rock posters, candles, stationery, doorknobs, mink-covered can openers, and other stuff. The pin was on a clearance table with other disasters that no one else had bought.

Joel immediately picked it up and said, "This is it. It's fantastic, really perfect. I love it."

I didn't know how to tell him that it was awful. "Listen, Joel. Are you sure your mother will like it?"

Looking at me, he smiled and said, "She'll hate it. Don't you see? She'll just hate it. It's perfect. She'll never figure out if I know how ugly it is or if I think it's beautiful. When she comes to see me or if I have to go there, she'll have to wear it. It'll look awful. And when I show it to my grandmother before I send it, she'll never know either. Those two don't realize a guy can have good taste."

"Is that your mother's mother?"

"No. My father's. But my mother and she are a lot alike. They think everyone has to be a certain way and that's it. I'm glad my father's not like that. He's cool. He listens to me when I talk, and he doesn't make me think the way he does. And I like the things he says and does. He's O.K."

"Wish mine was."

"Just don't let them get to you. In three and a half more years you'll be in college . . . or at least out on your own. Just try to survive until then."

"Joel, do you have trouble surviving?"

"Yeah, sometimes. But I'll make it. You too."

"It's easier for you."

"Why?"

"Well, your father's cool and you look O.K."

"What's that have to do with it?"

"It's easier if you look O.K."

"Marcy, looks don't matter."

Sure, that's what he always says. Maybe he's right, but it's sure hard to believe that when the rest of the world is skinny.

The salesperson came over to ask if we needed any help. He probably thought that since we had been standing there for a while talking we were casing the place for a giant robbery, or at least planning to shoplift an ugly toilet seat.

I smiled at him and said, "My friend here has just decided to purchase one of the lovely items. We were just wondering if it is a one-of-a-kind piece. It's for his mother, and he wants it to be something that's unusual, that everyone else won't be wearing."

The salesperson looked down at the pin in Joel's hand, tried not to smile, and said, "I'm quite positive that you're not going to see that on too many people. That's an unusual pin."

Joel nodded. "Yeah. It's a special pin for a special person. I try to pick presents that

122

are like the people they're for. This pin is just right for my mother."

"She must be an unusual person."

Joel nodded his head again, and we headed for the cash register. Neither of us said anything else until we got out of the store. Once we did, Joel turned to me and said, "Very unusual," and we both started laughing so hard that we couldn't stop.

Finally I wiped the tears out of my eyes and said, "Joel, let's go back to my house and get some lunch. My mother will have the police out for us if we don't get back, and if we stay here the cops'll get us for disorderly conduct."

Wiping his eyes, Joel said, "You're right. There probably is a law against laughing. And if there isn't, they'll make one. Don't worry, if we get arrested for being happy, my father will defend us. I can see it all now." And he jumped up on an empty chair. "Ladies and gentlemen of the jury. You were young once. Surely the crime of these poor misguided children, laughing in a public place and having fun, is something that you once did. They will learn as they grow up. Young Mr. Anderson has already begun reforming. He now dreams of becoming a school principal, and is currently taking mean pills in preparation thereof. Ms. Lewis, on the other hand, will not easily reform. She has pledged to follow the example of that awful Ms. Finney and become a fantastic English teacher, who teaches kids no prepositional phrases. But, dear ladies and gentlemen of the jury, Ms. Lewis will atone in time. Just yesterday, in her jail cell, she asked for a grammar book to read while eating her bread and water."

I jumped on the chair next to Joel's. "We throw the fate of these two misguided innocents on you. Remember, justice must be tempered with mercy."

At that point, one of the shopping center rent-a-cops came over and said, "Listen, you two. Very funny. Now get down and move on."

So Joel and I hopped down and headed off.

When we got to my house, my mother was sitting on the steps playing with Stuart. When he saw us coming, he ran over yelling, "Marcy. Joel. What did you buy me?" My mother looked over at us. She looked very lonely all of a sudden.

I walked over, hugged her, and said, "What's for lunch? We're starving."

She smiled. "Is Joel staying?"

I nodded.

Stuart kept saying, "What did you get me?"

I looked down at him. "Nothing."

He started to cry.

Another family scene.

Joel kneeled down, put his hand on Stuart's shoulder, and said, "Stuart, come on, be good. You don't get a present every time you want one. It's not like that."

Stuart held Wolf up. "Kiss Wolf."

Joel laughed. "Don't be silly, Stuart. I hardly know Wolf."

Mother, Joel, and I started to laugh, too. Stuart didn't understand, but he began to smile. We all went inside and had lunch. Stuart and Joel had peanut butter and banana sandwiches and Mother and I had tuna fish, Weight Watchers style.

After lunch, Joel, Stuart, and I went out to the park and played with a Frisbee. Afterwards both of us sat on a bench and watched Stuart swing.

"He's a good kid. Sometimes I wish I had brothers and sisters."

"I think it would be nice to be an only child."

"Don't you like Stuart?"

"Yeah. But I always get blamed when he does something wrong. And lots of times they're nicer to him than me."

"I think you should be nice to him. He's a good kid, and he's fun. The thing with Wolf is funny. I bet he gets lonely sometimes. That's why Wolf is his friend. Doesn't he know any kids his own age?"

I thought about all that for a few minutes and said, "He knows some kids at nursery school and some of the neighborhood kids, but he's alone a lot. They make fun of him because of Wolf. That dumb teddy bear."

"I like him. He likes you a lot. You should give him a chance."

"It's hard in my family to just be friends with any of them. They always ask me to do things."

Stuart came running. He wanted to play Frisbee again.

Joel, Stuart, and I played until dinnertime. Then Joel left to go home, and Stuart and I headed back to our house.

Chapter 17

I woke up the next morning with a stomachache and a horrible headache. At first I thought that I was doomed to some horrible sickness that teenagers always catch on television shows.

Then I remembered. Today was the date of Ms. Finney's hearing. By night I would know if she was going to be back or not.

I got out of bed and dressed. My stomach and head still ached, but I figured I'd survive, and anyway, if I told my mother, she might not let me go to the hearing.

So I went downstairs. My father had already left for work. My mother was sitting down at the table, reading the paper.

"Marcy, look, there's a lot about Ms. Finney in here."

She handed me the paper, and I sat

down to read it. There was interesting stuff in it, all about how Ms. Finney had gone to a progressive college and how she was currently going for a master's degree. The paper said that during college she had been active in drama productions, had been on the literary and humor magazines, the yearbook and newspaper staffs, and had helped organize group-dynamics activities. She had also been involved in college demonstrations. And she'd been elected to a national honor society.

"She's a bright, interesting woman. I hope that she comes back as your teacher."

"Me too."

"Turn to the 'Letters to the Editor' page. It's all about Ms. Finney."

I turned to the page. There were lots of letters, about fifty-fifty for and against. The people supporting her tended to use "Ms." in their letters, and the ones against her would call her "Miss Finney." One of them was from Mrs. Alexander, Robert's mother. She wrote that Miss Finney was warping young minds and was unpatriotic and should be fired. There was also a letter from Joel and his father, standing behind Ms. Finney, saying that she was a great innovative teacher.

"Mom, did you see Joel and his father's letter?"

"Yes, Marcy. Keep reading."

I skimmed the rest of the page; Ms. Finney had shown us how to read quickly for important facts. Glancing at the bottom of the page, I saw a letter signed by my mother. It said that as the president of the PTA and as the mother of two children, she was profoundly interested in the state of education and that she felt that Ms. Finney had helped the students to learn English and to learn to like themselves.

"Oh, Mom. Why didn't you tell me? It's such a nice letter. Oh, what's Dad going to say when he sees this?"

"He saw it this morning. I showed it to him."

"Did he yell?"

"No. He said that he didn't approve but that I had to do what I thought was right. Then he said that my place was in the home, not being political, and that he hoped I would come to my senses."

"Then what happened?"

"I told him that my place was wherever I wanted to be, and he left and slammed the door."

"Oh, Mom."

"You know, Marcy, I feel very good about this. I feel much stronger. And guess what else?"

"What?"

"I've decided that I'm going to get out and look for a job or maybe go back to school. What do you think?"

I smiled. "I'm happy."

"Me too."

The phone rang. I ran to answer it. Joel was on the other end. He'd seen my mother's letter and called to ask if he could come over and visit. I said, "Sure," then hung up and went back to talk.

"Joel's coming over."

"Good, I'm glad. He's nice, Marcy. I'm pleased that the two of you are going out."

"Listen, we're just friends. Don't send out wedding invitations yet."

My mother laughed.

The phone rang again. This time it was Nancy. She wanted to know if I could come over. I told her that Joel was on his way and we might be over later.

Standing near the phone, my mother said, "I'm so glad that you've made some new friends."

I nodded. "And they don't tell me all the time that I have to look like everybody else."

"They don't care about you the way I do. I'm your mother. I don't mean to hurt you. It would be so nice to see you thin."

"Please don't start. Come on."

We looked at each other carefully. Then I started to walk away.

"Marcy, I love you. Let me help you be all that you can. Please. I want you to help me, too."

I ran back to her, and we hugged each other.

When the doorbell rang, I ran to the door, opened it, and smiled. It was so good to see Joel.

He came in and talked to my mother and me, and then the two of us went over to Nancy's house and spent the day watching quiz shows and talking.

Joel walked me back to the house and told me that he'd see me at the hearing. I was getting nervous again just thinking about it.

Dinner at my house was another scene. My father refused to say anything through most of the meal. As he drank his coffee, he just stared at my mother and me. Finally, he started to talk.

"You know, it'll be great when that Miss Finney gets fired. It'll teach both of you not to get involved in bleeding-heart causes. Watch out for yourself, that's my motto. Don't always be on the side of radicals. It'll get you nowhere."

I bit my lower lip to keep from saying anything. He wasn't going to bother me. I didn't want to let him.

He continued, "Lily, you've managed to get involved. I don't understand you anymore. You've always been such a good wife."

My mother frowned and started to clear the table. "Martin, I'm still a good wife, probably better now that I say what I think. Please, let's not fight. I've made up my mind."

Grumbling, he picked up his coffee.

Beginning to help clear the table, I said, "What time are we leaving for the hearing?"

He said, "I've decided. We're not going."

Turning around, my mother said, "Don't worry, Marcy, I still have a set of keys to the car. We're leaving in half an hour."

My stomach started to hurt, and I started to shake.

"So now you're upset. Well, it serves you right, young lady. You've managed to disrupt the whole household."

Dropping the dishes on the floor, I ran upstairs. I couldn't stop shaking. My mother followed.

"Come on, honey, please stop. Please. It's going to be all right."

She held me and rocked me back and forth. "Marcy, please. Honey. Do you want to talk about it? What can I do? Please. I promise I'll get you help. We'll both go to someone for counseling. Even if your father doesn't like it, I'll go to work to pay for it. Please. I'm sorry."

The phone rang. My mother picked it up. It was Nancy. She handed me the phone, but I shook my head. She took it back.

"Nancy, Marcy can't talk to you right now. Could I please speak to your mother?"

She smiled at me and waited for Mrs. Sheridan to get on the phone.

"Hello, Sara? Listen, we're having a little problem here. Are you going to the hearing? Good. Could you possibly pick Marcy and me up? . . . No, there's nothing wrong with the car . . . Yes . . . Martin's being impossible . . . O.K. We'll see you in about ten minutes." She hung up.

I had calmed down a little. Seeing how calm my mother was helped me. I couldn't believe it. Smiling at me, she said, "Go wash your face. Let's get going."

Once I got my face washed, we headed downstairs.

My father was standing in the living room, holding on to a small piece of the car engine. He held it out to us. "If you're planning to use the car, you'll have to figure out where this goes."

My mother glared at him. "Martin, you know what you can do with that." Turning to me, she said, "Come on, Marcy, let's wait outside."

We waited on the steps. In a few minutes Nancy and her parents drove up. We got into the car. No one said much. It was obvious that things were tense.

Finally, Mr. Sheridan said, "I want you girls to remember that Ms. Finney may not win. If that happens, she'll probably have to take it to court. This is just a school hearing, you know. Be prepared for anything that happens."

Mrs. Sheridan said, "I've heard that she's gotten the backing of the American Civil Liberties Union."

My mother nodded. "I just hope she wins. It's very important."

No one said anything else.

As we got close to the school, we saw that the place was jammed. People were picketing. Others were just standing around. There were even television cameras.

Mr. Sheridan let us out and went to look for a parking space. I'd never seen the high school so crowded. An interviewer came up to my mother. "I understand you are president of the PTA. We'd like you to make a statement."

My mother smiled at the man and said, "I feel that Ms. Finney is a fine teacher and should be where she belongs, in front of a classroom." Someone booed. Another person cheered. I could see that my mother was a little shaky. The interviewer left.

"Good work, Ms. Lewis. You did that well." We turned around and saw Joel, who was smiling. Phil was standing with him.

My mother laughed and said, "Thank you, Joel. I'm happy to have a chance to do my part."

Phil said, "We'd better head in if we're going to find a place to sit."

"Why don't you go in and save seats for the rest of us?" my mother suggested. "We're still waiting for Mr. Sheridan."

So Nancy, Phil, Joel, and I went inside.

Finding seats, we looked around. Joel asked me how everything was going.

"Not so good. The scene at my house tonight was horrible. You wouldn't believe it."

Joel looked at me. "I thought it might have been bad when I didn't see him here tonight."

The Sheridans and my mother joined us, so we stopped talking about it.

All of a sudden everyone in the auditorium started to turn around. Ms. Finney was arriving. With her were three people, two men and another woman. One was the man who had played guitar with her in class. The other two carried briefcases and looked official.

I was so nervous, I felt that I couldn't breathe. But it was great to see Ms. Finney. She looked very tired, though.

They sat down in the front row in a special section. Then the Board of Education members came out and sat down at long tables in the front of the room. The school board president, Mr. Winston, pounded his gavel and said, "There will be no disruptions, nor will there be any cameras used. If these rules are not followed, this hearing will be closed."

Then they began. First they had to talk about old business. The budget was discussed. Bus routes were argued about. Teachers' salary negotiations were mentioned. Finally, after what seemed like hours, Mr. Winston said that it was time for the new business.

Everyone was absolutely quiet. Mr. Winston said that there were several items on his agenda to cover. I couldn't believe it. They still weren't going to get to Ms. Finney. My stomach was beginning to kill me.

They named teachers who were resigning, approved teachers who were replacing them; decided on when we would make up the days missed; and then Mr. Winston said, "We are now ready to begin discussing Miss Barbara Finney. I would like to remind everyone that this room must remain orderly."

Mr. Stone got up to speak first. He said that Barbara Finney had been a problem since she got to the school; that she dressed strangely; that her teaching was not traditional, and that he never would have hired her if Mr. Edwards had not left suddenly. Miss Finney's students, he continued, were rude to him and were getting wild. Moreover, as a veteran he found her not saying the Pledge of Allegiance an unpatriotic and misguided stand. He finished up by saying that he did not want her in his school anymore.

Several people cheered. Mr. Winston pounded his gavel and warned everyone to remain quiet. Then he called Ms. Finney up. He asked her to reply to Mr. Stone's charges.

She stared straight ahead and began. "I don't think it's a crime to dress differently. I never dress immodestly at school, nor do I tell the students how to dress.

"As for teaching differently, that's very true. I'm not at all ashamed of that. I'm hopefully teaching human beings to communicate with one another and to love and respect the English language. I try to do it in ways that will interest and excite students. Everyone complains that children can't and don't read. Well, my students are reading, and their writing has improved. Just check their records. The results are there. Isn't that what's important?"

She paused to catch her breath. Her voice got softer. "As for the Pledge of Allegiance, I choose not to say it. I salute the flag each morning as a symbol of what this country is supposed to be, but I can't say the Pledge. I am sorry to have to say that I don't believe this country offers liberty and justice for all. I will continue to work toward that end, but until I see it happening, I will not say the Pledge. I am a good

American. I care about the country and the people in it."

Then she sat down.

We began to applaud. Mr. Winston pounded his gavel. "This is your last warning. One more outburst and I'll clear this auditorium."

He continued. "The Board has at its disposal independent evaluation reports on Miss Finney. They are satisfactory. Therefore, our decision will be based on Miss Finney's refusal to say the Pledge. At this time, the Board will adjourn, and will return with its decision as soon as possible."

The Board members got up and went into some meeting room.

Everybody else got up to stretch or go out for a smoke. Joel grabbed my hand and said, "Come on, Marcy. Let's try to see Ms. Finney."

We pushed through the crowd. Joel was good at getting by all those people. Finally we made it through the lobby, and outside Ms. Finney and her friends were standing near a curb, smoking cigarettes and talking to reporters. I was scared to go up to them, but Joel moved right in.

"Hi, Ms. Finney."

She smiled. "Oh, hi, Joel, Marcy, how are you?"

I just nodded my head and started to cry.

She leaned over and put her hands on my shoulders.

"Marcy, it's not easy, I know. But everything will work out all right."

"Hey, Ms. Finney. Did you hear? We got suspended."

She nodded her head. "So I heard. Your plans were very supportive. I appreciate that. But you know it's necessary that you take responsibility for your actions. Are you sorry now that you're suspended?"

I said, "It's worth it."

She smiled. "I'm glad. Hey, have you read any good books lately?"

Joel and I told her about the books that we were reading.

She looked at both of us and said, "I miss all of you very much."

"We miss you too," I said.

"I want all of you to understand that no matter what happens, I care about all of you and want you to do your best to learn."

"Aw, Ms. Finney. Don't worry. You'll be back." That was Joel.

Tears started to roll down her face. "Please. I want you to remember all the things I've taught you."

I touched her arm. "I'll remember. Don't worry."

She tried to smile. "Marcy. You've grown so much. I'm so proud of you."

A lot of other kids were standing around, waiting to talk to her, so we said good-bye and walked back to our seats.

Joel and I talked about how we hoped that the Board would say that Ms. Finney should stay. We knew Joel's father was for her, but didn't know about the others.

My mother was sitting near us. She was talking to Mrs. Sheridan. Even though Mom looked tired, she seemed calmer than she'd been in a long time.

The Board members started to come back. So did everyone else, including Ms. Finney. Her face was streaked with tears.

Once everyone was seated, Mr. Winston started pounding the gavel again. He looked like a carpenter.

The room hushed. I had all of my fingers crossed. I looked over at Joel. His eyes were closed; his fists clenched. I was having trouble breathing again, and my heart felt as if it was going to explode.

Mr. Winston stood up and held on to a piece of paper. He looked down at it and began reading. "There is no question in the Board's mind that Miss Barbara

141

Finney has a sincere desire to educate youth. It is also apparent that she has the support of many of the children in her class. We appreciate this, but also wish to state that the majority of the Board does not approve of her stand." He paused and took a sip of water.

I started to cry. It was all over.

He continued. "Although we do not as a group approve, there is a legal precedent to support her stand. We therefore reinstate Barbara Finney to her position as a teacher in our school system."

The room exploded. Everybody started screaming and yelling at once. Joel and I were jumping up and down. I looked over at my mother. She was yelling and clapping her hands. I couldn't believe how happy I was. Everything was fantastic.

All of a sudden, people in the front started sitting down, and you could hear "Shh, shh." I looked to the front and saw Ms. Finney standing next to Mr. Winston, who was wildly pounding his gavel.

The room quieted down again. Mr. Winston said, "Miss Finney wishes to make an announcement."

She stood there, looking very pale.

I thought, You tell them, Ms. Finney. Tell those fools off.

She looked very shaky, but then she sort of smiled and said, "I want to thank everyone who has supported me. I've tried to always be all that I tell my students to be. Therefore, I felt it necessary to follow through and take a stand concerning the Pledge. It was important to me that I win, but it is even more important that I can be an effective teacher. This community has been split on this issue so badly that I doubt that I can ever walk back into my classes and be effective. Therefore, I feel that I must resign, effective immediately." Finishing, she turned and ran out of the room. Her friends followed.

I felt as if someone had hit me in the stomach. Stunned, I could feel the tears begin again.

I heard Joel. "That fink. That rotten fink. I hate her."

I turned to him. He was crying. "I don't believe it. Marcy, how can she do it? I trusted her."

My mother called over, "Marcy. Joel. Please come here." Mr. Anderson was with her.

"We want to take you both out for sodas and a talk."

"I don't want to go."

"Me neither."

My mother spoke in a voice that I'd never heard her use before. "Want to or not, you must listen to us. There's no use in falling apart. That never solves anything. I've learned that."

So the four of us said good-bye to the Sheridans and Phil and went to a diner.

Joel and I sat across from my mother and Mr. Anderson. Neither of us said anything.

My mother began. "I know how you both feel. It's very hard for me to accept. But maybe she was right. It would have been very hard for her to stay."

"True," Mr. Anderson said. "It might have been impossible. You know everyone would be watching for her to make the slightest mistake."

"Marcy, look at how much this whole situation has helped both of us grow," my mother said.

I thought about that.

"I hate her," Joel said. "How could she do it."

Joel's father put his hand on his son's arm. "I know this is very hard for you. You trusted her and you feel that she's left you . . . just like your mother did. That's it, isn't it?"

Joel nodded his head.

I looked at him and then at his father.

How I wished my father could understand so much.

I thought about what Mr. Anderson had said and how Joel must feel. I reached out and touched him too. "Joel, remember when Ms. Finney said that we should continue to learn no matter what. That's what we have to do. She cares about us. She just had to do what was best for her."

I thought about what Ms. Finney had said about remembering what she taught us. "Hey, Joel. Remember that part in *To Kill a Mockingbird* where Atticus says to Jem that you can't understand someone until you've walked around in his or her shoes for a while. That's what you've got to do."

Joel smiled. Ms. Finney had had us write about that, and Joel had written about Mr. Stone. He had said that if he walked around in Mr. Stone's shoes he'd have a lot of blisters, because everything about Mr. Stone rubbed him the wrong way.

"Yeah. Maybe you're right. I'm too tired to think anymore about this. I want to go home."

So we all got up and left. Once I got home, I went right up to bed. There was no way I could deal with anything else.

Chapter 18

It's been a month since the hearing, and a lot of things have happened.

My mother is registering for night courses at a nearby college. And she doesn't give me ice cream whenever I get upset.

Joel and I are very close. It's not a romance, but it's a good friendship. You have to start someplace.

I no longer think I'm a blimp. Now I think I'm a helium balloon.

I still hate my father. He hardly ever says anything to me anymore. He and my mother talk a lot, but he just looks at me and shakes his head.

I'm flunking gym for the year. Our new English teacher is giving us a test on dangling participles.

I still see Mr. Stone in the hall. I'd throw

up on his head if I were tall enough.

Stuart still has a thing about Wolf. Now he's refusing to go to nursery school unless Wolf also gets registered as a student. I can see it all now. When Stuart graduates from high school, he'll probably have Wolf right beside him. They'll award Wolf a diploma and he'll be elected "Bear Most Likely to Succeed."

I'm going to a psychologist. She's very nice, and she's helping me. It's different from Smedley, but I think I'm learning a lot.

Joel's father said that he heard that Ms. Finney was going to graduate school to get a doctorate in something called bibliotherapy. That's counseling using books and writing. That sounds good. Maybe someday I'll do something like that.

Yesterday I looked in the mirror and saw a pimple. Its name is Agnes.

Author's note

It's hard for me to believe that it has been thirty years since the publication of my first novel, *The Cat Ate My Gymsuit*.

Growing up, I loved to read and dreamed of becoming a writer. I practiced my autograph for the time when I would have a book to sign.

By 1970, I was an eighth- and ninth-grade teacher and had not written fiction since graduating from college three years earlier. I was very involved in teaching. . . . lesson plans, papers to grade, working with my students. There didn't seem to be much time to begin a novel. . . . and I wasn't sure what I wanted to write.

1970 was a time of political strife. There was the war in Vietnam. People questioned whether or not we should be involved. Lives were being lost. There was a lot of disagreement. There was the civil rights movement. People of all colors weren't being treated equally or fairly. Individual rights were challenged by the government.

1970 was not an easy time for me. Stopped at a stop sign, my car was hit from behind by a police car. Six days later, on the way to a doctor to check out injuries from the first accident, a drunk driver collided head-on with our car. My head smashed against the windshield, shattering the glass. One hundred stitches in my face. . . . minimal brain damage. . . . I had to quit teaching and work on relearning reading and handwriting.

I felt lost, not sure of what to do next.

I decided that with the way my luck was going, if I wanted to write, I'd better start before I got run over by a truck.

I started the book. I restarted the book. I wrote. I rewrote.

I wrote what I knew best. . . . about a heavy girl with a tyrannical father, a nervous mother, an annoying younger brother, and a poor self-image. . . . and about a bright and creative teacher, one who was politically active.

Finally *The Cat Ate My Gymsuit* was finished in 1973 and published in 1974.

I, who had practiced my autograph since

the second grade, had a book to sign!

Thirty years later — 2004 — the book is still being read in classrooms. . . . at home. People come up to me at conferences and tell me that their lives were changed, that they didn't feel so alone after reading *The Cat Ate My Gymsuit*. Students send fan letters. One generation introduces it to the next generation.

Penguin Books has deemed it "A MODERN CLASSIC." I am honored. I am happy.

Thirty years later. Some of the same issues, political and personal, are still present. The U.S. is again in a questionable war. There are debates about equality. . . . about individual freedom. . . . about the judgments of political leaders. . . . about our own judgments.

Thirty years — that's a long time. . . . It went by very quickly.

I got older.

Marcy Lewis, the main character, remains thirteen.

I hope that she. . . . and I. . . . continue to speak to readers for a very long time.

— Paula Danziger

The employees of Thorndike Press hope you have enjoyed this Large Print book. All our Thorndike and Wheeler Large Print titles are designed for easy reading, and all our books are made to last. Other Thorndike Press Large Print books are available at your library, through selected bookstores, or directly from us.

For information about titles, please call:

(800) 223-1244

or visit our Web site at:

www.gale.com/thorndike
www.gale.com/wheeler

To share your comments, please write:

Publisher
Thorndike Press
295 Kennedy Memorial Drive
Waterville, ME   04901